Tears were streaming down Macy's cheeks.

She wasn't his problem, Tanner reminded himself. But for the life of him, he couldn't walk away from her.

"I want to fix this all for Colby and I can't," she said. "He's only seven. I have to find a way to help him get past his grief and his anger." She covered her face with her hands. "I'm mad because I don't know what to do for Colby." Her eyes closed and she shook her head.

"Macy?" he asked gently. He needed to let her continue, to talk it out.

"There are days I wonder if Colby would be better off with someone else, with anyone but me. But I'm his family. We have each other."

"Yes," he said, "and in the end, that matters."

"But what if I'm not a mom? What if I can't do this?" She looked young standing there next to him, her green eyes troubled.

He had to say just the right thing.

* * *

Lone Star Cowboy League: Boys Ranch
Bighearted ranchers in small-town Texas

Brenda Minton lives in the Ozarks with her husband, children, cats, dogs and strays. She is a pastor's wife, Sunday school teacher, coffee addict and sleep deprived. Not in that order. Her dream to be an author for Harlequin started somewhere in the pages of a romance novel about a young American woman stranded in a Spanish castle. Her dreams came true, and twenty-plus books later, she is an author hoping to inspire young girls to dream.

Books by Brenda Minton

Love Inspired

Lone Star Cowboy League: Boys Ranch
The Rancher's Texas Match

Lone Star Cowboy League
A Reunion for the Rancher

Martin's Crossing
A Rancher for Christmas
The Rancher Takes a Bride
The Rancher's Second Chance
The Rancher's First Love
Her Rancher Bodyguard

Visit the Author Profile page at Harlequin.com for more titles.

The Rancher's Texas Match

Brenda Minton

Special thanks and acknowledgment to Brenda Minton for her contribution to the Lone Star Cowboy League: Boys Ranch miniseries.

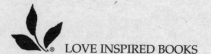

Recycling programs for this product may not exist in your area.

LOVE INSPIRED BOOKS

ISBN-13: 978-0-373-81936-2

The Rancher's Texas Match

www.Harlequin.com

Printed in U.S.A.

Pure and genuine religion in the sight of God the Father means caring for orphans and widows in their distress and refusing to allow the world to corrupt you.
—*James 1:27*

Dedicated to the workers who tirelessly serve,
helping children and families in need.

Chapter One

The Silver Star ranch was one of the prettiest, most peaceful places Macy Swanson had ever experienced, from the stately oaks that lined the fenced drive, to the white-sided, two-story home. Behind the home was a red barn. In the background were the three cabins that made up the Lone Star Cowboy League Boys Ranch.

The Silver Star, on first glance, looked as if it might be a family ranch. On second glance, a person noticed the boys. From ages six to seventeen they were the reason the ranch existed in its current state and the reason she had come there. Because one of those boys was hers. Her nephew, Colby.

As she parked under the shade of a twisted old oak tree, she caught the tears before they could fall. She took a deep breath, to let go of the pain, the grief. The guilt. It took more than one breath.

It took several. It took a swipe of her finger under her eyes to brush away the evidence. Even now, at the first of October and almost a year since the accident that had taken her brother and sister-in-law, the grief still sneaked up on her.

She missed her brother, Grant. She missed Cynthia, his wife. They should have been here, raising their son. Instead she was the one trying to fill their shoes after the crash that ended their lives. She was the one trying to put the pieces back together for Colby, only seven and still angry and hurt that his parents weren't coming back.

The guilt sometimes outweighed the grief because she didn't know how to help her nephew. She had always wanted children. Now she doubted she knew how to be a mom. After all, she didn't seem able to fix this one hurting little boy.

Someone tapped on her car window. She jumped a little, moving her hand to the steering wheel and managing to smile up at the man looking in at her.

Tanner Barstow. Wonderful. The rancher and volunteer at the boys ranch stepped back from the door as she pushed it open. He'd posed as Mr. January for the calendar the community put out as a fund-raiser for the ranch. The Cowboys of McLennan County calendar had been a hit, she'd been told. She had a copy hanging in her kitchen. It had been there when she moved in last winter, after the accident.

Her life had become segmented, broken in two distinct halves. Before the accident. After the accident.

Before the accident she'd been engaged to Bill, an attorney in Dallas. She'd been a librarian, managing several libraries in the Dallas metro area.

After the accident… She was still trying to find the person she was after the accident. She now lived in Haven, where she was a librarian at the local library, a substitute teacher at the high school and a volunteer at the Silver Star. Most important, she was the aunt of Colby, determined to find a way to make that little boy smile.

"Are you okay?" Tanner asked as she stepped out of her car.

He was a full head taller than her five-feet-eight inches. He was rangy, lean and powerful. His jeans rode low on his hips. The button-up shirt tugged at his shoulders. His dark chestnut hair was wavy, and she could tell that when it curled, it bothered him. Maybe because he couldn't control it. He seemed to be a man who liked control. Dark blue eyes caught her attention. He was giving her a skeptical look, as if he was positive she couldn't be okay.

And maybe she wasn't. Maybe she was so far out of her depth here in this small town that she didn't know if she would sink or swim. Mostly, she felt as if she was sinking.

"I'm good." She cleared her throat and gave him a smile that wavered; she felt it tremble a little.

"It's going to get better. Give him time. Give yourself time." He said it like he meant it. She nodded and closed her eyes, against the brightness of the sun and against the pitying look he was giving her.

"I know," she finally answered, and she thought it sounded as if she meant it or believed it. She added a hopeful smile for punctuation.

"Come, watch him ride. We're in the arena today. He's doing great."

His hand brushed her back to guide her in that direction. The touch was brief, but the comfort of the gesture couldn't be denied. She could really use a friend. She could use a hug. She shook off that thought as one that went too far. After all, she'd made friends in Haven, through work and through the Haven Community Church. She wasn't alone. Not completely.

But the idea of a hug wasn't wholly without merit. What would Tanner Barstow, vice president of the local Lone Star Cowboy League, self-made rancher and horse trainer extraordinaire, do if she asked him for a hug? He'd probably do the man-hug, quick and from the side, and then head for the hills.

Movement in the arena caught her attention. She watched as the boys, all younger, rode around the enclosure. They kept their horses in an easy lope, right hands on the reins, left hands at their sides.

"What are they doing?" she asked as they walked in that direction.

They stopped a few feet from the white, wood fence of the arena. She kept her attention focused on Colby. He was such a tiny little guy, with his mom's dark hair and his dad's green eyes. The ranch hand in the arena called all the boys to the center. A young teen stood next to him. The boys rode their horses and lined up so that boys and animals were facing the ranch hand.

"They're practicing showmanship, for Western pleasure classes at local events. It takes control for the horses, and for the boys."

"This is such a great place. I'm so glad it was here for Colby. I don't know what we would have done."

He nodded, acknowledging the comment. His gaze remained on the boys and the men working with them. "It's the best. It was truly inspired. When Luella Snowden Phillips started this ranch, she probably didn't realize how long-lasting and far-reaching the ministry would be. But it's been here for seven decades. I just wish we had more room and could take more boys."

"They were praying about that at church last Sunday," she offered. "Someone mentioned that boys had been turned away. And wouldn't it be an amazing thing if no child was ever turned away from this program?"

"That would be amazing." He walked away from her, moving a little closer to the fence. "I heard Colby had a hard time last weekend."

He shifted, settling his gaze on her just momentarily before turning his attention back to the boys in the arena.

Was that an accusation? Or was she just being unduly sensitive? Colby had been allowed a twenty-four-hour pass to go home with her. She'd had to bring him back to the ranch early.

"It's hard for him to be at home. I keep thinking that it will get easier, that he'll want to be there."

"Don't give up." He stepped away from her, heading toward the gate. "If you'll excuse me."

She nodded as he walked away. From the arena someone shouted. She saw the ranch hand who was working with the boys move quickly. As she watched, the boys dismounted and started tugging their horses away from the center of the arena. Tanner was through the gate, leaving it open in the process.

"Close that," he called back to her.

She reached the gate and closed it as she went through. The boy at the center of the ruckus was yelling at Jake, the ranch hand who'd been instructing them. The other boys, most of them under ten, were backing away as Tanner hurried to help. It looked like chaos about to be unleashed. The teenager who'd been helping was trying to get control of the nearly half dozen boys left to fend for themselves as the adults focused on the one youngster who was causing the problems.

The boy at the center of the trouble had hold of his horse and was backing away from the two men. The horse, wild-eyed and jerking to be free, kept moving. The boy held tight to the reins.

Colby hurried toward her, dragging his horse along with him. He had tears in his eyes. His friends didn't look much better.

"Hey, guys. Let's see if we can get these horses in the barn. We'll put them in stalls." She looked to the teen helper for guidance. "You're Ben, right? Do the horses go in stalls?"

He grinned, showing crooked teeth but a charming dimple. His hair was light brown, and his eyes were warm hazel. "Yes, ma'am. I can put the horses in the stalls."

"Why don't we do that?" She looked at the

group of boys surrounding her. Big eyes, sweet smiles. She glanced back in time to see that Tanner had hold of the poor horse being dragged about the arena.

"Come on, guys, let's see if we can have fun." She clasped her hands together as she stared at the expectant faces.

Colby didn't look convinced.

"Colby, what story do you like the best?" she asked.

That got his attention. That was their common ground. Stories.

"The one with the dragon slayer," he said as he reached for her hand, his other hand holding the reins of his pony.

"The dragon slayer it is." She only hoped she could remember the story she'd made up on a Saturday night when neither of them could sleep. She smiled down at her nephew. If she couldn't remember, he would help.

In the background she heard a young voice raised in anger. Or hurt. A calm, reassuring voice spoke; the words were lost, but the tone carried the meaning.

Macy felt that reassurance, even though it wasn't meant for her.

"The dragon slayer knelt in prayer, knowing his kingdom would stand forever and that it was a greater power than his own that kept them safe from the evil…"

Tanner stood just outside the open barn doors, unwilling to go in and interrupt. He'd taken Sam Clark back to the cabin where he lived and to the house parents, Eleanor and Edward Mack, who would make sure he was safe until he could regain control of his behavior.

The eleven-year-old had been at the ranch for six months. He was a good kid who had seen the bad side of life. The result was a lot of anger. Edward and Eleanor could handle it; with degrees in counseling, and their involvement in the local church, they were experts on the kids at the ranch.

Kids wanted people to connect with. Even when they fought the people who cared, they still wanted to be cared about.

Tanner got it. Until the age of ten he'd lived that same life. His parents had been abusive to each other and their children. They'd been drug addicts who couldn't hold down jobs. There hadn't been a safety net until the state sent the three Barstow kids to live with Aunt May in Haven, a community just on the outskirts of Waco. The move had saved his life. His older brother, Travis, had struggled a bit more and had lived at the boys ranch for a while. Their little sister, Chloe, hadn't been much more than a baby when they were sent to live with their dad's aunt May.

Young voices erupted as the story being told ended. He peeked inside the barn and watched as those five young boys moved closer to Macy Swanson, her nephew included. The little boy had recently turned seven. Colby's hand was on her arm, and he stood close to her side. From thirty feet away Tanner could see her nerves. It was easy to perceive that she was afraid to move, afraid to lose the thin thread of connection between her and her nephew.

But the story she'd been telling had enthralled the kids. They were still asking questions about the dragon and the dragon slayer. She was telling them about faith in a way that a kid could understand.

He didn't know Macy very well, but he had to admire how she could calm a group of rowdy boys with a story. If he was being honest, there were other things to admire, things a man couldn't help but notice. He sure didn't mind admiring or noticing. Sunlight danced through the center aisle of the barn, the beams of light catching in the blond hair that hung loose to the middle of her back. She was tall and classy. Beautiful, really.

And all city.

Things transplanted typically did better when

transplanted into a similar environment. That was what he knew from living in the country. A water oak didn't tend to do well in hot, sandy soil. Cacti thrived in the desert. That was just the way it was. City folks thrived in the city, and country people tended to stay in the country.

Macy looked up as he approached, her smile touching her green eyes with a warmth that took him by surprise. The boys remained circled around her. They had avoided the worst of Sam's outburst and had been entertained with a story; they were on top of the world. Even Ben had lurked at the edge, listening to the story.

Ben, fourteen, tall and lanky with a shock of light brown hair, had been at the ranch for two years. He was a good kid. He'd had one failed attempt at going home. He'd been adopted as a preschooler, and the experts said he had trouble bonding because of his early childhood. That made sense to Tanner. The boy was sometimes angry and tended to push away when he started warming up to people.

But he was doing better. They could all see that.

Time. For so many of these kids it took a lot of time to heal. With that thought, his gaze fell on Colby Swanson. The boy's parents had died in a car accident, and his grief had turned to anger that made him act out at school and be difficult to handle at home.

When a spot had opened, Macy placed him at the ranch.

"You boys get all of your stuff gathered up." Tanner let his gaze fall on Colby. The little boy was holding tight to his aunt Macy. "And maybe we can get Miss Swanson to finish her story, or read to you all when you have library time."

His phone rang. Rotten timing. He would have ignored it, but the caller ID flashed the name of the president of the local chapter of the Lone Star Cowboy League, an organization started over a hundred years earlier to help ranching communities. Since Gabriel Everett didn't call just to shoot the breeze, it had to be important.

Jake, about the best hand around, had entered the barn from a side door. The big bonus was that not only could he break a horse to saddle, he also had a knack with the kids on the ranch.

"Jake, can you and Ben go ahead and take these guys on down to Bea?" He didn't have to spell it out. Beatrice Brewster, the no-nonsense director of the LSCL Boys Ranch, ran the show. She'd watch the kids until she got the all clear from house parents Edward and Eleanor, who had their hands full with Sam.

Jake gave him a thumbs-up and started organizing the boys for the march to the main ranch house. Without asking, Macy fell in with Jake and the boys. She volunteered in the ranch office, helping with accounting. She'd also become pretty adept at finding donations and writing up grants. She didn't usually help with the kids. But at times like this, everyone pitched in and helped out.

"Gabriel, what can I do for you?" Tanner watched as the small troupe marched toward the big ranch house, and then he headed for his truck.

"Tanner, we need to have an emergency meeting of the League. Can you be here in about fifteen minutes? Bring Bea with you. And Katie will probably need to attend so she can take notes for the ranch."

"I'll be there." He glanced at his watch. "What's going on?"

"I'd rather make the announcement when you get here. Let's just say that some prayers are answered a little quicker than others."

Interesting. "I'll be there in ten minutes."

When he pulled up to the ranch, Bea was already on her way down the stairs. Tall and in her fifties, the former social worker for the state was all heart. She adjusted her glasses and smoothed her hair, turning to give a "hurry up" look to the person following her out the door.

Macy Swanson?

The two climbed in his truck, Macy opening the back door and getting in the backseat. Beatrice clicked her seat belt and settled her purse on her lap.

"Katie is staying to help Jake with the kids. I asked Macy to come with us to take notes. I'm going to want my own person there so that we have a record of our own." Beatrice shot him a questioning look. "Do you know what is going on, Tanner Barstow?"

Like he was one of her kids and someone had TP'd the house.

"No, Bea, I don't. I got the call the same as you."

"Gabriel said it's a good thing. But, Tanner, I'll have you know, I'm not a fan of surprises. Even of the good variety."

"I'm sure it'll be fine." He glanced in the rear-view mirror and caught a glimpse of Macy looking out the window, bottom lip caught between her teeth. He cleared his throat, and she shot him a look. "I'm sorry I put you on the spot back there. So, do you think you'd be interested in spending time reading to the kids? They enjoyed the story you told them."

"I'm not sure," she finally answered. "I mean, it would be good, wouldn't it? The boys enjoyed it. Colby enjoyed it."

He slowed to make his turn. "Think about it."

The Everett Ranch, owned by Gabriel Everett, was a big spread located between the Silver Star and Haven. Tanner parked next to a half dozen assorted trucks and SUVs. He got out quickly so he could hurry to the other side and open the door for the ladies. His dad hadn't taught him to be a gentleman, but Aunt May had. She'd told him someday he'd appreciate the manners she instilled in him. He'd be thankful.

He was, and he wished she was alive so he could tell her how much she'd meant to him and his siblings. But she'd passed about eight years ago, getting them mostly raised, all but Chloe, who had been not quite fifteen. May had at least seen Tanner's business get off the ground. She'd known they would be okay without her.

Eight years later Haven Tractor and Supply was well-established, and Aunt May's small ranch had quadrupled in size. He didn't mind feeling proud of that accomplishment. May had sold off land to get him through college. He'd put the family spread, the Rocking B, all back together for her. It had taken him a few years, buying back the land as it came up for sale or as he convinced neighbors to sell it back to him.

He opened the door for Bea. She stepped out, not needing the hand he held out for her. He reached to open the door for Macy, as well.

"Thank you, Tanner." Beatrice patted his arm, as if he wasn't thirty-two and just twenty years her junior. With Bea they were all kids.

The ladies preceded him to the house. He didn't mind. A few more minutes meant a little more time to think; maybe he might come up with some reason they were all being called to the Everett place for a meeting. But by the time they were shown to the library, where the meetings were held, he still didn't have a clue.

A gavel pounded on the table. Tanner sat back and gave Gabriel his full attention, but then his gaze shifted to the right of the league president. The man sitting in the seat of honor was Harold Haverman, attorney and member of the Lone Star Cowboy League, of which Tanner was vice president. It seemed to him that if there was something going on, Tanner should have been told ahead of time.

Tall, with a black Stetson covering his gray hair and metal-framed glasses on the end of his nose, Harold had presence. And he had a document in his hands that looked far too official.

"Meeting to order." Gabriel glanced around the group. He cited the date, the time, the emergency status of a meeting of the Waco district Lone Star Cowboy League chapter.

The formalities were taken care of with some seconds, a vote, and then on to new business.

"I would like to recognize our guest, Harold Haverman."

Harold stood, pushed the silver-framed glasses

back in place and shifted the papers he still held. He gave them all a look, serious as could be, no hints as to what this was all about.

"I'd like to thank you all for coming today. I know this is unexpected." He peered at them over the top of those glasses. "As you all know, we lost a respected member of our community. Cyrus Culpepper passed last week. I know several of you attended his funeral. Today I have the honor of sharing with you his last will and testament."

"What does this have to do with me?" Bea started to stand, but Gabriel shook his head. "I have children at home."

"Bea, this won't take a minute." Harold cleared his throat and shook out the papers. "If you'll just give me five minutes to read this. And then we can take care of the details."

He started to read. Silence held as the members looked from one to the other, clearly astonished. Tanner glanced across the table and made quick eye contact with Macy Swanson and got caught in those green eyes of hers. She looked wary and like she was pretty sure she shouldn't be involved. She also looked like someone still hurting. The grief for her brother had turned to pain for a little boy still missing his parents.

Listening as Haverman read the final will of one Cyrus Culpepper, curmudgeon and stirrer of the pot, Tanner thought that maybe they'd all just been tossed in the middle of a big old mess.

I, Cyrus B. Culpepper, am writing this on my deathbed with, per my doc of over forty years, only days or weeks to go. I may be about to meet my maker, but I am of sound mind and hereby bequeath the bulk of my estate to the Boys Ranch, as I was once a resident myself back when the ranch first started in 1947. Yes, that's right. I might be an old curmudgeon who can't tolerate a thing, but since I was once a troubled kid who was turned around by the Boys Ranch, I want to do something for the place. However, I have conditions. When I lived at the Boys Ranch, there were four other original residents who I lost touch with. I would like you to bring them together for a reunion at the ranch on March 20th, a party on my birthday for the 70th anniversary celebration of the Boys Ranch. That gives you six months. Now, now, quit your bellyaching— given all the newfangled technology, search engines and social media nonsense, you'll probably find them lickety-split. Though I never tried, so who knows? I suppose I've gotten a bit nostalgic in my old age and leave it up to you whippersnappers to do my bidding.

Oh—and one more thing. I had a son, John Culpepper, who I didn't get on with too well after his mother passed. We were estranged, but I know he had a child, a girl—Avery—who lost her mother. I heard, well after the fact, that my son died when the child was young. I have no idea what happened to her, and I'd like to invite her to the ranch to receive an inheritance.

If the terms of my will are not met, I've instructed my attorney, Harold Haverman, to bequeath the estate, minus a small endowment to the Boys Ranch, to Lance Thurston, a real estate developer, to build a strip mall bearing my name. Sometimes you have to provide the right incentive.

Now for the boring part. The "bulk of my estate" is to include my ranch house and all the outbuildings, livestock and land except for the cabin in which I grew up and the five acres of land it sits on. That cabin, five miles from the ranch on the outskirts of town, and land is bequeathed to Miss Avery Culpepper, to be given to her in March. I was a self-starter and believe everyone should be, but I also believe I did wrong by Avery and want her to have what she

likely would have garnered over the years as my granddaughter. The rest of my bank accounts and investments are bequeathed to the LSCL Boys Ranch.
Yours, Cyrus B. Culpepper

Everyone was talking at once. Outrage. Shock. The library fairly rattled with raised voices. Fletcher Snowden Phillips, last remaining kin of the founders of the boys ranch, was the loudest. He was crowing that the ranch was meant to be at Silver Star and nowhere else. For a man constantly trying to litigate against the ranch, that rang false.

Gabriel Everett pounded the gavel on the table, and a hush fell with just a few last-ditch remarks from those wanting to voice concern.

"It looks as if we'll need volunteers." Gabriel looked over the group that had gone suspiciously quiet. No surprise. Everyone had something to say until they were asked to contribute more than words.

Macy Swanson raised a tentative hand, and Gabriel gave her the floor. Tanner leaned back in his chair, wondering what she planned on saying…and why he was so interested to hear it.

Chapter Two

"I'll volunteer to help find one of the people on the list. If anyone needs use of the library computers, they're available. Social media is probably a good place to start searching." She made quick eye contact with the people at the table, and when she got to Tanner, she faltered. Their gazes connected and she felt her cheeks flush.

Gabriel Everett sat down at the head of the big table. He looked too relieved when Macy volunteered. And she felt a little apprehensive. She wasn't a part of this group, of this town, or their lives. Every single day she woke up in Haven she felt like a fraud. She could buy boots, show up at church, even cook a decent dessert for the monthly potluck. But she was as far from country as a person could get.

And she'd never been a part of a community, not a tight-knit place like this. People asked questions, they prodded, they wanted to be involved in her life and have her involved in theirs. She'd never been that kind of person. She'd grown up in a sprawling neighborhood, but she hadn't known her neighbors.

So why in the world had she raised her hand to volunteer? Because Gabriel had looked like a lost giant standing at the end of the table waiting for someone to say something?

Now that she'd opened her mouth to volunteer, everyone was staring. Tanner Barstow, blue eyes and too-handsome face, wore a frown as he studied her from across the table. She glanced at Bea, hoping for a little moral support.

Bea patted her arm and smiled big. "Well, there you go. We're all sitting here stunned, and Macy is jumping right in. Gabriel, give us that list again so that Macy can write them down, and we can figure out who is doing what here. It seems to me that we don't have time to waste. We need that ranch."

"And what if we can't find those four people and the granddaughter?" Fletcher Snowden Phillips stood. He was tall, middle-aged, with thinning hair and a scowl that could have put off the most well-intentioned person.

Macy shivered in reaction to his growling voice. As a lawyer, Fletcher knew how to back people down. And she knew that he had long wanted the boys ranch closed. She found that hard to believe, considering his grandmother Luella Snowden Phillips, along with the Lone Star Cowboy League, Waco Chapter, had started the boys ranch. His own father, Tucker, had been the *reason* for the ranch. A neighboring rancher had helped put Tucker back on the straight and narrow, and later on, mother and son had done what they could to save other boys.

"What if these people have passed, or are too sick or just unwilling to come to this event Cyrus wanted us to plan?" Seth Jacobs, a rancher from closer to Waco, asked. Macy had met him at the boys ranch.

Harold Haverman tapped the pages of the will on the table and stood, sliding the papers back into a folder. "If you don't find the people he has asked you to find, well, we'll cross that bridge when we get to it."

"I think the will clearly states that the property will be turned into a strip mall." Gabriel shook his head as he made the observation.

"That's a mighty big strip mall," Tanner drawled in that low, easy voice of his. He grinned at Gabriel. "I find it hard to believe Cyrus would do that to his pride and joy."

"It isn't for us to say what Cyrus would or wouldn't have done," Beatrice chimed in. "We have to make sure that ranch becomes the property of the League because we have boys waiting to be a part of our program."

"I get that, Bea, but it seems a little like a wild-goose chase to me." Flint Rawlings, foreman of the boys ranch, swept a large hand through his dark blond hair and then settled his hat back on his head. He rested his gaze on Fletcher. "And, Fletch, don't get all excited. The boys ranch isn't going to come to an end if we don't get that property. We still have the Silver Star."

Fletcher shook his head and then clamped his mouth closed. It was well-known around town that Fletcher used his legal might against the ranch. No one really understood why.

Gabriel cleared his throat. "We have five people to find, if you include Cyrus's granddaughter, Avery."

"And who are they?" Beatrice prodded.

Gabriel picked up a piece of paper. "Avery Culpepper, the granddaughter, and then we have Samuel Teller, Morton Mason, Edmond Grayson and Theodore Linley."

Bea coughed a little, and Macy saw her shoot a look in Tanner's direction. "Well, Gabriel, you should be able to help us find Theo."

Gabriel pushed the paper aside. Macy was lost. She didn't know these people or their stories. She waited, watching each person at the table as they reacted to the list.

"My grandfather and I haven't spoken in so long, I wouldn't recognize his voice on the phone. I'm not sure I'd know him if I saw him. And I doubt he wants to talk to me." Gabriel glanced around the room. "I have one volunteer."

"I'll look for Theodore Linley," Tanner offered into the silent room.

Gabriel gave a curt nod. "I appreciate that."

"I'll look for Avery Culpepper," Macy offered.

Next to her, Beatrice tapped her fingers on the table and hmm'ed. "Well, I have the most at stake. Or should I say, my kids do. I'll look for Samuel Teller and Morton Mason. It seems as if I might have a few emails or letters from former members. It might be easier than we think."

Flint, sitting closest to Gabriel, reached for the paper. "I guess I'll look for Mr. Grayson. That name is common, but I have a friend with the same last name."

Beatrice smiled big. "So, the good Lord willing…"

"And the creek don't rise," someone muttered from the other end of the table.

Bea shot the offending party a look. "I've been praying for a bigger place or for money to build more cabins. The church has been praying. God has opened this door, and I, for one, intend on going through it."

"Amen," Gabriel murmured. "When does the Triple C become the property of the boys ranch and the LSCL?"

Mr. Haverman looked at his notes. "Possession begins one month from the reading of the will. Although you understand if the stipulations of the will aren't met, you'll have to return the property and move the boys back to the Silver Star. And Miss Avery Culpepper will be allowed to move to her property in March. And, please, don't question me, because Cyrus had his reasons."

Gabriel closed his eyes and ran a hand over them. Finally he looked out over the group that had assembled. "And with that, we will adjourn the meeting. If any of you want to stay and plan how to proceed, feel free to use this room. I'm afraid I have another appointment."

With that, he picked up his briefcase and left.

Macy made eye contact with Bea. The other woman just shrugged and adjusted her horn-rimmed glasses but then turned her attention to Tanner.

"Well, Tanner?" Bea prodded.

The room had cleared, leaving only the four of them. Macy, Tanner, Flint and Bea. Tanner got up and headed for the coffeepot and Styrofoam cups.

"Coffee?" he offered.

He started pouring cups before anyone could answer.

"This Culpepper ranch is large?" Macy asked as she took the offered cup. She didn't mean to notice Tanner's hands, long-fingered, tanned, calloused, but when their fingers touched, she couldn't help it.

Flint laughed at the question, but his smile was genuinely friendly. "The Triple C is a big spread. The house has three wings. There are plenty of buildings. And there's room to grow."

Beatrice got up to make copies of the list of names. "And that property is going to be our new ranch. I'm just not willing to give up on this. Every day I get a call from the state. There aren't enough foster homes or residential facilities. Macy put Colby on the list last winter, and it took us several months to get him a bed. It breaks my heart each time we have to turn away a child in need of a home, or counseling."

Tanner stopped behind Beatrice and placed a hand on her shoulder. "We won't let you down, Bea."

He took one of the papers she'd copied and returned to his seat. Macy pulled out her phone and typed the name Avery Culpepper into the search engine. A slew of entries appeared. She held the phone up for the others to see.

"It isn't going to be easy, but it won't be that difficult. There are dozens of hits for the name Avery Culpepper. I'm sure you'll have the same experience with your names. And then it's a matter of tracking down the correct person."

"I hope it's that easy," Flint grumbled.

"Me, too." Bea stood. "I'm not sure what else we can do here today. I have a dozen boys waiting to be fed, and I guess some kind of chaos Tanner created before we left."

Tanner grinned. "Yeah, that's what I do, create chaos. But the kid whisperer, Macy, calmed them all down with a story."

Kid whisperer. She wished that were true. If it were true, she wouldn't be a failure with her own nephew. As they stood to go, Tanner stepped in close.

"He'll survive this." He said it with conviction.

"I'm sorry?" She looked up, unsure what he meant.

"Colby," he continued. "I know you worry about him, but give it time. He'll come around."

"I hope you're right." She prayed he was right. Because she didn't want to lose her nephew. For Colby she would stay in Haven. She would manage to be the person he needed her to be in this small town with people who commented, gave advice and offered help.

What other choice did she have? She'd given

up her life and her career in Dallas. She'd given up the fiancé who didn't support her decisions.

This was her new life.

As they left together, Tanner touched her back, a gesture that comforted. She was sure that was what he meant by the fleeting contact. But it did more than comfort her; it made her aware of his presence.

In all the months she'd been here, he'd struck her as a man who didn't get involved. He was a successful rancher and business owner. He sometimes showed up at the boys ranch. He rarely took time to socialize.

Today she was in a vulnerable place, worrying about Colby and missing her brother. Tomorrow she would be back to normal and Tanner's touch, his kind words, would make sense.

Tanner strode through the doors of the Haven Tractor and Supply. His sister, Chloe, looked up from the counter and smiled. He felt immediately on edge because she was wearing that look, the one that spelled trouble for him. She wanted something. And he'd probably give in and get it for her. If he could.

"Been busy?" he asked as he walked behind the counter. He saw that she'd been doodling on a piece of paper. Pictures of dresses. The wedding variety of dress. He cringed. She was twenty-four and old enough, but he didn't think she was ready. As an older brother he doubted he'd ever be ready to see her walked down the aisle, by either himself or their brother, Major Travis Barstow.

"Not real busy. Larry has a customer on the lot, looking at a tractor. Or a stock trailer. I'm not sure which." She tapped the pencil on the counter and sneaked a look at him.

He pretended not to notice, but he almost couldn't hide a smile. She was pretty, his sister. Dark hair in a ponytail, she was all country with beat-up boots, faded jeans. She made it all feminine with a lacy top she'd probably spent a day's wages on.

"Are you selling off steers this weekend?" She hopped up on a stool and slid the doodles under the cash register. Like he hadn't noticed.

"Are you buying wedding dresses?"

She turned a little pink. "No. I'm a girl. We dream about weddings."

"You've only been dating Russell for a few months."

Her smile dissolved. "He's a good guy, Tanner. He's made mistakes, but he's got a job, and he's trying to make things right."

"I know that. I'm willing to give him a chance, but I'm not willing to let him hurt you."

Her smile returned. "I've been thinking that

maybe you could let him volunteer at the Silver Star. They're going to need help moving, and it would give you a chance to get to know him."

"I'll talk to Beatrice. But, Chloe, I'm not going to put up with nonsense when he's around the kids."

"I know and I appreciate that. Tanner, he made mistakes when he was young. His parents' divorce really upset him. He did things he shouldn't have. But that isn't who he is."

"He stole a truck and a stock trailer full of cattle."

"He was seventeen. He hasn't been that person in a long time."

"People in town have their suspicions."

Before he could finish, Chloe slid off the stool and closed the distance between them. Yeah, he was in trouble. She'd always known how to work him. With a soft smile, she kissed his cheek and then patted it.

"You're the best big brother a girl could have."

"And you always say that when you get what you want."

She didn't move away. Her blue eyes glistened with tears, and his own throat tightened in response because he knew she was going to drag them back into the past, into memories she didn't have because she'd been too young.

"You've been taking care of me for a long

time," she started. "Since I was a baby you've been the one feeding me, changing my diapers and keeping me safe."

"How would you know? You were a baby."

"Travis told me. And Aunt May. She said she had a hard time getting you to let go and just be a kid. You were always the one. You took care of us. And then you took care of May."

"Do you have a point?" he asked, his voice more gruff than he'd intended. It didn't seem to bother her. No, not his little sister. She smiled and dug her heels in, intent on some emotional rabbit trail.

"Yes, I have a point. Find someone to love, Tanner. You're not getting any younger, you know. And I'm past the age of really needing a caretaker."

"Thanks for that reminder of my advancing age."

She grinned at that. "It's the truth. You are getting a little long in the tooth. But, seriously, you'd make an amazing dad and a great husband. So why not let yourself be loved? Stop thinking you have to be there for everyone else, and let someone be there for you."

"Words of wisdom?"

She scooted around him and headed for the door. "I am wise. I'm also right. It's time for you to find a wife. Travis is happy in California. I'm eventually going to get married. And then you'll be alone in that castle you've built."

"It isn't a castle."

"It's your kingdom," she countered. "Fill it with kids."

She left, and he didn't have a thing to say in response to her lecture. It was almost closing time. He walked to the front door and watched as his salesman and mechanic, Larry, walked past the building to an old farm truck. The customer was old Joe Falkner, known to be worth millions. Joe still drove a truck he'd bought new a couple of decades ago. He lived in a house that appeared to be falling apart. But he raised some of the best Angus in the state.

He joined Larry as Joe drove off.

"Don't tell me Joe is thinking of getting a new stock trailer."

Larry laughed and pulled a stick of gum out of his pocket. He'd been trying to quit smoking for six months. So now he chewed gum. A lot of gum. He offered a piece to Tanner.

"Yeah, he's going to have to buy a trailer. The floor rotted out of his. The guy who normally fixes it said no more, he isn't fixing that trailer again."

"Did you close him on one?"

Larry shook his head. "He won't turn loose of

a dime. He said in 1970-something he could get that trailer for, I don't know, a ridiculous amount."

"I guess if he decides to haul some cattle to auction, he'll come back and buy a trailer."

"Knowing Joe, he'll go hire some drovers and herd those cattle to the auction like they did a hundred years ago."

"Don't give him that idea." Tanner glanced at his watch. "I'm going to take a drive. You'll be here for a bit?"

"Yeah, anything you need me to do?"

"Yeah, pray. We've got six months to find some people, or old Cyrus Culpepper's place is going to be paved over."

"I'd heard rumors about a crazy will. You can't pave over that many acres, and Cyrus hated those types of developments."

"Tell that to his will."

Larry adjusted the bent-up cowboy hat he always wore. "He was an ornery old cuss. It's hard to tell what he was thinking, but I'm sure he had some kind of angle when he came up with this plan."

"I'd sure like to know what it was. If I don't get back, will you close up?"

"You got it, boss." Larry headed back to the building.

Tanner didn't really have a plan when he left, but he found himself heading up the drive of the

Triple C. It wasn't too far from his own spread. When he pulled up, he saw another car in the driveway. He got out of his truck, surprised to see Macy sitting on the hood of her car looking at the old Culpepper place.

For a long minute he stood watching her. Her blond hair was pulled back with a headband, and sunglasses perched on the end of her nose. She looked out of place in jeans, boots and a plaid shirt, as if she was trying to fit, but she didn't. She was city, from her manicured nails to the way she stepped around mud to keep it from getting on those boots of hers.

He admired that she wanted to blend, that she wanted to transplant herself in this community for the sake of a little boy who had already lost too much.

Admiring was as far as he wanted to let his thoughts take him on a sunny day in October when his sister was looking at wedding dresses, his brother was currently on temporary duty somewhere in the Middle East and Cyrus had strung them all up by their toes, asking for something that might be impossible. "I came to pray," she finally said without turning to look at him.

The words took him by surprise, but they weren't uncomfortable the way they might have been if someone else had said them. She was simply stating a fact.

He closed the distance between them.

"I came to take a look around. I haven't been here in years. I don't know if anyone has been up here. Cyrus kept a loaded shotgun, and he made it pretty clear he'd shoot first and ask questions later." He grinned at the memory of the old guy.

"He didn't like people?"

He leaned a hip against the hood of her car, leaving a good bit of space between them. "I guess he liked people okay. He just didn't want anyone messing around up here. He must have liked people, because he's making a big donation to the LSCL Boys Ranch."

"He isn't making it easy."

"I guess that's true. But we'll work it out. Like most of us, Cyrus had baggage. I never knew he had a kid, let alone a granddaughter. I didn't know he'd lived at the ranch."

"There are several Avery Culpeppers in the area."

It hadn't taken her long to get started. He hadn't even thought about where to start his search for Theo Linley. He doubted Gabriel would be much help.

"We'll find them all," he assured her. Or maybe he was hoping to assure himself.

They sat in silence looking at the big house with the pillared front porch. There were three wings. Plenty of space for kids to run and be kids. He'd looked over the will, and it said they could go ahead and begin moving. It would take weeks to get the process started. There would be supplies to purchase, as well as volunteers to organize. A place like this meant more of everything. More staff. More furniture. More food. More time. But it would be worth it.

It would be good to have the boys in this house so they could celebrate Christmas in their new home.

"I should be going." She slid off the hood of her car.

"Me, too." He paused, watching as she dug her keys out of her pocket. "Have you thought about what I asked you earlier? About reading to the boys?"

She glanced away from him, her hand going up to brush strands of blond hair from her face as the wind picked up a bit. "I don't know."

"Something troubling you?"

"No, not at all." But the worried look in her green eyes said that something about the offer did worry her.

"It isn't something you have to decide on today. The library as it is will be packed up and moved over here. We just got it put together. Now we'll have to take it all apart and do it all over again."

She moved to her car, and her hand settled

on the door. "I can help with that, with getting things packed and then getting the new library organized."

"That would be good. I hate to overwhelm you, since you're new to the area, but you might have noticed if we get a willing volunteer, we use them."

"I don't scare easily. And I don't mind helping."

He reached past her to open the car door, the way Aunt May had taught him. A hint of something soft and floral, like wild roses on a spring day, caught and held him a little longer than was necessary or safe.

Chloe would have told him to stop living his life off a list he'd made twenty years ago. He couldn't. That list had served him well. It had taken him from the gutter to the life he had now, and someday he'd find a woman to share that life with him.

He closed the car door and watched Macy drive away in her little economy car, and he smiled. She wasn't at all the woman he was looking for. But something about her made him think about finding someone.

Chapter Three

Macy juggled her purse, book bag and keys in order to get her front door unlocked. As much as she wanted to just crash, she had more work to do and she was going to need a cup of coffee to get her through the rest of the day. It had been a few days since the reading of Cyrus Culpepper's will. She'd been substituting at the Haven high school, so she hadn't had much time to think about finding Avery Culpepper or even going out to the Silver Star.

Entering the house, she was met by silence. It was peaceful. But lonely. Colby should be here. He should be running to the kitchen to grab a snack, plopping in front of the TV to watch his favorite afternoon shows.

But then, in a perfect world her brother and sister-in-law would be here to greet him. Macy would still be in Dallas. Maybe she'd even be planning her wedding.

Instead she was standing in her brother's kitchen fighting the familiar doubts that had assailed her since she'd learned that he'd named her guardian of his son. In the beginning she'd believed they would make it, she and Colby. His anger had proved her wrong. It had proved she wasn't a parent, or even something close to a parent. She was twenty-eight, single, and hadn't even begun the process of thinking about kids.

Grant's and Cynthia's deaths had changed everything. For Colby. And for her.

It had amazed Macy that her brother had found his way to the small town of Haven. Their mother, Nora, had insisted he could do better if he stayed in the city. He would have moved up, made more, had a nicer home than the remodeled craftsman house with its large front porch, complete with porch swing.

Grant and Cynthia had been happy in Haven.

She worried that she didn't have it in her to be the small-town librarian, mother of Colby.

She turned on the coffeemaker and found her favorite mug. As she waited for the water to heat, she stood at the window and looked out at the small but wooded lot behind the house. Not a high-rise in sight. No sirens in the distance. Not a sound could be heard.

She missed Colby.

The ready light flashed, and she put her mug under the spout and pushed the button. Coffee poured into her mug. She opened the book bag that she'd brought home from school, and as she pulled out her organizer she noticed another book. She tugged it out, trying to decide where she'd picked it up and when. Yes, she'd been distracted today. She didn't think she'd been *that* distracted.

A note fell out of the book. She picked up the yellow piece of paper. A creepy, crawly feeling shivered down her spine.

The book was a middle grade book about a ranch. There was nothing remarkable about the title or the story. She set it down and turned her attention to the note. The feeling of apprehension eased.

Could you read this to the boys? Thanks, Tanner.

How in the world had the book gotten in her bag? Maybe when she'd stepped out of the room to make copies? But surely one of the students would have told her. She thought about the fifteen English literature students. No, they wouldn't have told her. All that aside, why would Tanner Barstow have a sudden desire to get her involved with the boys at the ranch? She couldn't even raise her own nephew.

Every single day she questioned why she was in Haven. She'd given up her career, her friends and her fiancé to be here for a little boy who only wanted his parents back.

She slid the note back into the book.

Maybe Tanner thought that if she spent more time with children, she would grow into the role of Colby's mom. That made sense because Tanner seemed to be a natural with children. He'd practically raised his own sister. He was the type who would get married, have a half dozen kids and never miss a step.

Macy worried that she didn't have that parenting gene. There were days that she loved the idea of raising her nephew, of someday being the person he ran to at the end of school, eager to tell her about his day. There were more nights that she lay awake, scared to death that she would never be able to fill that place in his life, and that he would never want her to be that person.

Beatrice had told her to take her time. In family therapy she'd learned to give him space and to not react when he pushed her away. It was hard, because every time he pushed her away, her heart took it personally.

When it hurt, like it did just then, she reminded herself that her pain was nothing compared to Colby's.

Her coffee was finished. She put a lid on the

thermal mug and grabbed the book Tanner had left for her. She had thirty minutes to get to the ranch. She'd promised Bea she would put some finishing touches on the ranch library, and she wanted to apply for another grant.

When Macy pulled up to the main house of the Silver Star, Beatrice's car was in the drive. Flint, the ranch foreman, was just walking down the front steps. He tipped his hat in greeting but went on, heading for the barn. Macy got out of her car and strode up to the house. Beatrice met her at the front door.

"Hey, Macy, I wasn't expecting you today."

Macy held the book out, and Bea took it, perplexed, her eyes narrowed as she studied it.

"What's this for?" Bea asked.

"I thought you might know. Tanner must have brought it to the school." She handed over the note.

"You didn't see him leave it?"

She shook her head. "No. I found it in the book bag I carry."

Bea motioned her inside. "That doesn't sound like Tanner. He doesn't do things willy-nilly like that."

"He asked me if I would read to the boys. I told him I'd have to think about it. I thought maybe he left it, hoping I'd say yes."

Bea led the way to the big kitchen at the back of the house. "Would you like a cup of tea?"

"That would be nice."

Bea put the teapot on to boil, and then she leaned against the counter, still giving the book her full attention. "Tanner should be here in a bit. We're going to see what we can find on our missing ranch alumni. You can ask him if and why he would leave a book for you. But if he did do this, don't feel as if you have to do what he's asking. I think you already do enough."

"I love doing what I can for the ranch, Bea. It's my way of giving back. You all rescued us. I'm not sure what would have happened to Colby if he hadn't gotten a spot here."

"I think you would have found him help. Go easy on yourself, Macy. Colby isn't the only one who has suffered. You lost your brother."

Unexpected tears burned at the backs of her eyes, and her throat constricted. Macy nodded, because if she opened her mouth, she might cry.

Bea placed a comforting hand on her arm. "Give yourself time to grieve. I think you have a tendency to go full throttle, fixing things. Some situations need time."

"I know. I'm just afraid. What if I can't be the person Colby needs me to be? What if he never gets over being angry? Eleanor Mack and I have discussed this several times. We understand anger and sadness at the loss of his parents, but it seems like the anger is magnified, and we don't know why."

Bea poured water in two cups. The fragrant aroma of herbal tea filled the air with hints of cinnamon and clove.

"I would agree with Eleanor. Colby is an especially angry little boy. But give it time. We'll figure out what is going on. Once we get to the root of the problem, we can start working on making the two of you a family. I know you're afraid you can't do this. We all feel that way when we are looking a problem head-on and thinking that this is our future. In time you come to a place where you realize you've survived it, and that, through it all, God made you a little stronger."

"Thanks, Bea. I hope you're right."

Bea chuckled, "Haven't you been told? I'm always right."

"And if she isn't, she'll find a way to convince you she is." Katie Ellis, in her twenties and receptionist of the boys ranch, entered the room. She got a cup and added a tea bag before pouring water.

"Katie, you know I'm always right." Bea pushed the sugar jar to the pretty blonde receptionist. "Oh, did I tell you that Pastor Walsh is coming by for Bible study with the boys? He has a new video series he wants to do with them."

Katie turned a little pink at the mention of the Haven Community Church pastor. "I'll make sure the meeting room is ready."

"That would be good. And you might offer to help him out." Bea grinned as she made the suggestion.

"I would, but I have to do laundry tonight." Katie headed for the door with her tea. "I'm going to head home. Is there anything else you need?"

"Nothing at all," Bea called out to her. And then to Macy, "That girl. Pretty as they come and sweet, but she's never really dated."

Dating, the last thing Macy wanted to discuss. She smiled and reached into her purse for the information she'd found on the many Avery Culpeppers.

"I found all of this last night. Maybe one of these will be Avery Culpepper, granddaughter. A few of them even live in Texas."

"You've been busy," Bea said as she looked over the list.

"I don't have much to do in the evenings."

Bea looked at her over the top of her glasses. "That's going to change when we get Colby home to you."

"I hope so, Bea. I really hope."

"It'll happen sooner than you know. I realize the two of you had a rough visit when he tried the weekend pass. But that was a big event, going home for the first time since coming here. There are a lot of memories, a lot he has to deal with. We'll try another pass soon, but for now we'll stick with day passes. He might do better with a few hours just to let him get used to being at home with you."

Macy must have made a face, because Bea patted her hand. "And that will give you a chance to get used to being the mom. He's going to need you, Macy."

She nodded, unable to give voice to her concerns. Booted footsteps interrupted the conversation. A moment later Tanner appeared in the kitchen. He was tall and broad-shouldered, ruggedly handsome, and for the better part of the year Macy had lived in Haven, he'd ignored her.

She could think of several reasons. Folks in small towns weren't always eager to welcome outsiders. Or maybe he didn't like that she'd made a mess of her relationship with Colby. He was protective of the kids on the ranch. She couldn't fault him for that.

"Are we having a meeting about our missing alumni?" He cut a path to the coffeepot and poured himself a cup, taking a whiff before adding sugar.

"It's a couple of hours old, probably a little on the bitter side," Bea informed him. "And, yes, an impromptu meeting. Macy got the surprise you left in her bag."

He turned, eyes narrowed as he looked from Bea to Macy. From that look, she knew he hadn't left the book.

Tanner leaned against the counter, not sure what to say to the two women who obviously thought he should know what they were talking about. He barely knew Macy Swanson. And he didn't make a habit of forming relationships with parents of the boys at the ranch. "Surprise?"

Macy pushed a book across the counter. He reached for it and gave it a long look. "Never seen it before."

She handed him a note with handwriting that definitely wasn't his. "This was attached."

He shook his head. "Again, I've never seen it before, and that isn't my writing."

"But you asked me to read to the boys." Macy's voice trailed off at the end, and she took the book back from him. "Who else would have done this?"

"Interesting question. But I just saw Pastor Walsh on the front lawn because he was told the boys want Bible studies on Friday afternoons. That's the first I've heard of that. Not that our boys aren't good kids, but they don't typically reach out to the local pastor wanting more church. More often than not, they complain about Sunday and Wednesday services."

Bea rubbed a finger across her chin and hmm'ed. "You know, I got a note next to my phone, like someone had left a message after talking to Pastor Walsh. It said he was interested in spending more time here with the boys and thought that perhaps Katie Ellis could help lead a Bible study with the boys. Of course I called him and asked when he'd like to do this."

"And here I was going to blame you, Bea." Tanner sat down next to the older woman.

"Well, it wasn't me, Tanner." She gave him an arch look over the top of her glasses.

He winked at Bea and then glanced at Macy. She sat with her gaze lowered, focusing on the book and not on him.

That gave him a few seconds to study the woman sitting across from him. A curtain of blond hair fell forward, slightly hiding her expression. She was slim and graceful; even her hands seemed delicate. Delicate but capable.

He cleared his throat and cleared the thoughts from his mind. "But now that you have the book, are you interested in reading to the boys? I've lost track of the ages, but I think we have several under the age of ten who would enjoy a little quality time with you. Colby being one of them."

"I'll read to the boys. We'll combine reading

with a lesson on how to use the library, and they can also help me start packing it up."

Bea clapped her hands together and shot him a beaming smile. "That sounds like a great idea. And I think this will give you some real quality time with Colby. He does love your stories. He talks about them, you know."

Macy's expression changed, her teeth worrying her bottom lip. "He always seems to draw back just as I think we're getting closer."

"Maybe he's afraid of getting close?" Tanner offered. "I remember when we first came to Aunt May. We'd been on our own, and suddenly there was this woman wanting to be involved in every moment of our lives. It wasn't easy to let her in."

"But he wasn't used to being on his own. He had parents who loved him and cared for him."

Bea sighed at the reminder.

"Yes, and then they were gone and you were there trying to fill their shoes. It hasn't been easy for either of you," Bea said, her arm around Macy's shoulders. "Now, Tanner, what brings you to the ranch this late in the day?"

"I wanted to arrange for the group of us looking for the lost residents to meet for dinner tomorrow evening at the steak house. I'm buying. We can look at any notes we've found and see what we need to do next."

"What time?"

"Six okay for everyone?"

"That sounds good," Bea said as she gathered their cups.

Tanner headed for the door, but then he remembered one other item on his list. "Oh, I forgot something."

Bea set the cups back down on the counter. "What is it?"

"Chloe wants to see if Russell can have a job helping out around here. I understand if the answer is no."

Bea laughed at that, taking him by surprise. "That girl can still wrap you around her little finger."

"Yes, she has a gift," Tanner acknowledged. "And she thinks I need to get to know the man she plans on marrying."

"We'll find him something to do. And try not to worry. We all know Russell. We know his past. After all, Tanner, the boy spent six months here."

"Of course. I just don't want any problems for you or the ranch."

"Don't you worry about us, we know how to handle young men like Russell."

Yes, if anyone knew how to handle Russell, it would be Bea. As he started to turn to go, his gaze landed on Macy. He didn't know what to say to her about the book and the note. Someone obviously wanted to push her into spending more time with Colby and the other boys at the ranch. Maybe Bea? Could even have been Flint or Jake.

Maybe he would ask Jake. He'd been there yesterday. Maybe he'd overheard Tanner ask Macy to help out, and he'd taken off with the idea in order to get her over here more often.

But the book and story time were low priority. The LSCL Boys Ranch needed Cyrus Culpepper's property. Still, as Tanner left the Silver Star, the Culpepper place wasn't on his mind. Instead his thoughts had turned to Macy Swanson and the strange turn of events that had her front and center in his life.

Chapter Four

The print of the grant Macy had typed up blurred a bit as she stared at it. She rubbed her eyes and leaned back in her chair. She'd been at the Silver Star since shortly after three, and she had three hours to go until the dinner at the steak house. If she hadn't agreed to the plan yesterday, she would back out and go home. But she had volunteered, and she wasn't canceling on people who were counting on her.

Things might seem a little brighter if she hadn't woken up that morning to a car that wouldn't start. She'd walked to school from her house. After work, Katie Ellis had given her a ride to the ranch. Macy would have to see if the other woman was still around to give her a ride back to town.

All in all it had been a long day. The kind of day that deserved another cup of coffee. Or a really long nap. And she was getting neither of those things. Instead she was sipping on a cup of herbal tea that Beatrice had brought her, something to soothe her, she'd been told.

A light rap on the door interrupted her musings. She smiled at the woman standing in the opening, her auburn hair pulled back. A floral shirt stretched tight over her belly. For a few months Josie Markham had tried to hide her pregnancy. Or maybe the young widow had been in denial. Her husband, a county deputy, had been killed in the line of duty. Only after his death did Josie learn that she was pregnant.

The two of them, Josie and Macy, had bonded immediately. They were both grieving, both trying to figure out the next step in their lives.

"Are you busy?" Josie asked as she stepped into the room and lowered herself into a chair. She was petite and even now seemed to be all belly.

"No, not really. I'm writing a new grant for a playground. But I have to decide how to word it. I'm trying to have faith that we'll get the Culpepper place. That changes things a bit."

"I guess that would complicate the grant process."

"Yes, a bit." Macy slid the grant paperwork into the filing cabinet and locked the drawer. "How are you feeling?"

Josie shrugged, but she briefly looked away and dashed a finger under her eye. A sign she wasn't as great as the chipper smile she always managed to show the world might indicate.

"I'm good." She sighed, and her hand went to her belly. "Good, meaning I'm waking up each morning. I'm moving forward, even though sometimes I feel like I'm stuck in quicksand."

"Josie, I'm so sorry." Macy reached for Josie's hand and gave her fingers a light squeeze. "If you need anything…"

The smile reappeared. "I know. And the same goes for you. We're quite a pair, aren't we? Neither of us planned parenthood this way. How's Colby doing?"

"I'm not sure. When I see him here, he seems fine. But when I tried to take him home, he was lost and then angry."

"He has been through so much for someone so young. Give him time."

"It's been a year, Josie. What if he needs more than I can give him?"

"What do you mean?"

Macy closed her eyes just briefly. What did she mean? How could she put these thoughts into words? "I worry that I'm not the right person to raise him. Would he be better if there was someone else, and I just went away?"

Josie leaned forward and placed a hand on her

arm. "Oh, Macy, don't. He needs you. He might be pushing you away, but in time he'll let you in."

"I hope so. And if that isn't the case, I hope God will show me what our next step is."

"Colby was always a good little guy." Josie sat for a long moment, looking out the window of the tiny office Macy used. "Maybe there's something else, something more. Does he say anything in therapy or their group sessions?"

"Not really. They've had a hard time getting him to open up about that night. I understand. Sometimes I'd like to brush it under the rug and pretend it didn't happen. But he's been stuck in the 'anger' stage of grief for so long. I just worry we won't get him to acceptance."

"And on top of that worry, now we have Cyrus's will to contend with. I don't know why his lawyer didn't try to talk him out of it."

"Do you think he could have talked him out of it?" Macy asked, already knowing the answer.

"Not a bit. And now I have to run. I'm helping Abby and John Garrett with the boys in their cabin. We're having a cookout and game night. But Bo Harrington is attending, and his son, Christopher, is already a pill without his parents there to make it worse."

Macy knew a little backstory, that Christopher Harrington was sixteen and spoiled. The state juvenile office had placed him at the ranch, and his parents were still determined to get him out.

"Have fun. I heard he waxed the windows of Abby's car. And he's pulled a couple of the other boys into his antics."

Josie groaned as she stood. "He's rotten. I think he has potential if his parents will learn to allow him to suffer consequences. See you later. And let me know how it goes with the meeting and the big hunt."

"Of course I will." She smiled and waved to her friend. She had thirty minutes to work in the library. She wanted to start organizing things for the move. With the goal of moving at the end of the month, Bea was in overdrive, trying to get everyone and everything organized.

The library would be one of the easiest rooms to pack. It was fairly new and already somewhat in order. The rest of the ranch, she shuddered to think of that process. Decades of accumulation and living and only a month to box it all up.

As she wandered about the lovely old room with the high ceilings and dark stained woodwork, she heard footsteps in the hall. Light footsteps. Not the heavy booted footsteps of one of the hands or the soft swish of Bea's sensible shoes.

She turned and caught sight of a slip of a boy, his dark hair mussed and his sneakers scuffing back and forth on the wood floor, as if he wasn't sure of his welcome. She knelt and held out her arms.

Colby ran into her embrace.

"Hey, sweet guy, what's up?" She wrapped her arms around him, wishing she could take away all of his pain, all of his anger. She would. She'd do it in a heartbeat because she knew she could process it, figure it out and move on. She had been moving on for the past year. Losing her brother, Grant. Losing her fiancé, her job.

But gaining Colby.

If only she could find a way to help him move on.

He shuddered in her arms, and his hand raised to swipe at tears rolling down his cheeks, dampening her sleeve. She tried to pull him back against her, but he stiffened, unwilling to have the embrace a second longer.

"Are you okay?" She stayed on her knees, her hands on his arms.

He nodded, but his green eyes swam with tears he was fighting to hold back. She bit down on her lip, trying to think of the right words. A mom should know what to say. A mom would know how to help him. She closed her eyes and admitted her failings in this area.

"Colby, I want to help you. I want to make it all better. If you could just tell me."

He shook his head, but he stepped a little closer.

"I love you," she whispered close to his ear. She brushed a kiss across his head, and he didn't move away.

"I love you, Aunt Macy." With those words her heart grabbed hold of hope.

"Did you sneak away from the cabin?"

He nodded and again swiped at tears that threatened to fall.

"Did someone upset you or hurt you?" Stupid question. Of course he was upset and hurt. But was this a new hurt or lingering pain?

It was like trying to put together a puzzle, but without all of the pieces. How she wanted all of the pieces! She wanted him whole. Sometimes she saw glimpses of the Colby she'd known before the accident. But the glimpses were fleeting.

He sat down on the floor in front of her, and she took that as an invitation and sat next to him.

What would a mom do? She desperately wanted to think like a mom, be a mom. She scooted close, but she didn't put her arms around him. She waited, knowing he needed time.

"Diego called me a big baby."

Diego, not much older than Colby. But with a different story and different baggage to work through.

"He's wrong," she told her nephew. "You're tough. Really tough."

"Ben took up for me. He told Diego to be nice, but Diego said that I'm not nice to you."

"You are nice to me." She covered his hand with hers. "We're going to make it through this."

"Because we're family now. That's what Eleanor says."

Eleanor Mack was counselor and house mother of Cabin One. Macy smiled and told herself to thank the other woman.

"Yes, we're family." She wanted to hold him. He smelled of the outdoors, of hay and livestock. He had red cheeks from playing in the sun. He was everything to her.

"I have to go." He stood, looking down at her with such a serious expression. For a moment she saw his father in him. Grant's seriousness. Her heart ached at the thought. "I'll walk you back."

He reached for her hand. It might as well have been her heart.

"Eleanor says I can have a pass to go to church on Sunday."

"I like that idea." Macy glanced down at the little man leading her through the house.

"Me, too. Do you think you can tell me another story?"

"I'm sure I can."

"Ben says you're going to read stories to us. He said he'd come with me."

She surprised herself by smiling. "That's fine."

"He's not too old for stories?" Colby asked as they walked out the front door. It was warm for the first week of October, but a light breeze blew, bringing country scents of cut grass, livestock and drying leaves.

"No. We're never too old for stories."

"That's good." They walked along the path to Cabin One, Colby swinging his hand that held hers. "Ben said we're going to move to another ranch. I don't know if any of us want to move. We like it here."

"But moving can sometimes be good. There will be more room for more boys at the new ranch."

Colby stopped walking and looked up at her, his green eyes narrowed against the glare of the sun. "But if they come here, it means there's something wrong in their homes."

"That might be true, Colby. But it's good that there's a place for them to go."

He continued walking, his hand still holding tight to hers. "But it would be better if moms and dads…"

"If they never went away?" she asked quietly.

He nodded, but he didn't answer.

"You're right, that would be better." She kept walking, trying hard not to give in to the tears burning her eyes. "I'm not going anywhere."

He didn't answer.

She left Colby with Eleanor. That moment, walking away from him, was as painful as the first day she'd left him at the ranch. The difference was that this time he hugged her goodbye. That first day he'd walked away without a word, without even looking back.

That parting hug gave her hope.

When she got back to the main house, Katie Ellis was waiting to give her a ride to the meeting where they would hopefully find that it would be no trouble to track down a few men who hadn't been seen or heard from in decades.

"How was Colby?" Katie asked as they pulled up to the restaurant.

The Candle Light, Haven's claim to fine dining, was on the main road. The building with the stone exterior had a long, covered porch with rocking chairs and potted plants. The parking lot was crowded. Typical for a Friday night in Haven.

"He's good," she answered Katie. "He was upset with Diego, but that's to be expected when you have so many kids living under one, or three, roofs. He hugged me goodbye."

Katie pulled the keys out of the ignition and gave her a quick and easy smile. "He's such a sweet boy, and he does love you."

"I know. And I love him. I hope he knows how much."

They got out and headed for the entrance to the restaurant. A dark blue Ford truck pulled up to the building. Macy knew that truck. She knew the man getting out, adjusting the cowboy hat he wore so naturally.

And it was just as natural to take a second look. But that was all she was doing, looking.

Tanner tipped his hat to the two ladies standing on the sidewalk of the Candle Light.

"Looks as if we're the first to arrive," he pointed out for no good reason. "I have the back room reserved, so we won't have to answer a million questions. I know people in town want to know what is going on. Until we have real answers, I'd prefer to keep things quiet."

Katie stepped through the door he opened for them, leaving Macy to slide in, brushing against his arm. He leaned in a little, just enough to catch the scent of wildflowers. "We've been getting calls at the ranch," Katie responded as he led them through the already crowded restaurant. "I'm not sure what to tell people."

"Tell them we'll release a statement to the local paper."

He stopped at the door to the private meeting room to wait for Macy. She'd stopped to say hello to the Macks, counselors from Silver Star, who were having a rare evening out. They waved when they spotted him.

He'd lived in this small town long enough to know that an innocent gesture had just been turned into a connection between himself and Macy. Because he looked like a man waiting for a woman, not a man merely holding the door the way he'd been taught.

He disliked small-town gossip, the constant speculation, pairing people up, marrying them off if they were seen having a cup of coffee or even walking in the same store. A few years back he'd dated Nina, a secretary at Fletcher Snowden Phillips's law office. She'd left town for a job in Houston. Neither of them had felt the need to keep the relationship going.

But the town had practically had them married off.

Macy parted from the Macks and hurried to join him.

"You didn't have to wait," she assured him as she slipped past him into the meeting room.

"I didn't mind."

She glanced up, her smile tipping her lips and crinkling at the corners of her eyes. "Oh, I think you did. You looked cornered, standing there with the door held open."

"I'm not sure why you think that," he countered, his hand going to her back to guide her to the table. There was an easy back-and-forth between himself and the woman who had taken him by surprise several times lately.

It was easy to touch her. Too easy.

He pulled a chair out for her. She accepted the gesture, sitting and scooting herself in as the door opened, and they were joined by Gabriel Everett, Beatrice and Flint. Fletcher followed them in. Tanner hadn't expected to see him at this meeting. It seemed the local lawyer had developed a habit of showing up uninvited.

It wasn't that Tanner disliked the other man. It was just that Fletcher did things that got under a person's skin. Although he should have felt a connection to the boys ranch, he seemed more often to be in favor of shutting the place down. He found fault with the boys, tried to pin petty crimes on the kids and turn them into juvenile delinquents, and he had opposed several grants that Macy had gotten for improvements.

It stood to reason that if Fletcher could find a way to keep them from getting a bigger property, he would. Or maybe he'd like to see them move after all. Tanner thought there might be a legal matter that would turn the Silver Star property over to Fletcher if the boys ranch closed or was no longer there.

Before he could say anything, a waitress entered with glasses of ice water and a coffeepot.

She smiled big as she surveyed the small group, but then she went to work, handing out water, filling cups and setting menus on the table.

After she left, Gabriel pulled a piece of paper out of his pocket. "I guess this isn't a meeting of the LSCL, so we don't have to call to order. Fletcher is here because he thought we might need his advice."

Gabriel shot the lawyer a look that said he didn't buy it. But Fletcher ignored the glance. He was probably used to making enemies.

Beatrice squeezed the lemon into her water and stirred, the spoon clanking against the edge of the glass. "I haven't had a chance to start digging too much. But I do have some information on a few of our men. I'm sorry, Gabriel. I don't know much about your grandfather."

Gabriel's slim smile completely disappeared. "Yeah, neither do I. In the past we've looked, but we haven't been able to locate him. And after a while we stopped trying."

"I'm sorry." Bea stopped stirring. "Gabriel, it's no shame that your grandfather was at the ranch. Tanner's brother, Travis, was there, and look how he turned out. The ranch has a purpose. It turns lives around and gives young men an opportunity to make something of themselves."

"Not every life can be saved." Fletcher said it quietly, smoothly. "And some just bring trouble to our town. I'd like for Haven to be more than the community that supports a ranch for troubled boys."

Flint practically growled. "Fletcher, I can show you to the door if your purpose here is to cause problems."

Fletcher held up hands of surrender. "I'm not. I'm just making a statement."

Flint picked up his menu. "Keep your statements to yourself."

"I've found several promising leads on Avery Culpepper," Macy offered.

The waitress returned, a notepad in hand. They ordered and she left again, closing the door behind her.

Macy stopped twirling the silver bangle bracelet that circled her slim wrist. "I have an Avery in Dallas, one in Austin and two in Houston. Those are the most promising leads, although I've also found one or two out of state."

Beatrice went next. "I think Samuel Teller will be easy to find. I have a letter from about ten years ago. It seems he did turn his life around, and he wanted to contribute to the ranch." She made a point to stare Fletcher down until he turned a little bit red. "I tried to call the number in the letter, and it's been disconnected. But I think it won't take long to locate him."

A phone rang. Katie pushed aside the notebook she'd been taking notes in and dug around in her purse. She gave them all an apologetic smile and hurried out of the room. When she returned, it was to gather up her things.

"I have to leave. My cousin is in crisis. Macy, maybe Bea or someone can give you a ride home?"

"Of course. For that matter, I can walk. It's only a few blocks, and the weather is great."

"I'll see you all Sunday at church."

She left, and the meeting continued until their steaks arrived. An hour later they were leaving. To Tanner it seemed as if they had a chance. And that meant the ranch had the chance to expand and bring in more boys.

Bea had left early, but she'd parted letting them know she'd had a phone call that day asking her to take another boy. She'd put the child on the waiting list because she didn't have a spare bed, and she already had close to twenty boys waiting.

Tanner was climbing into his truck when he noticed Macy walking away from the restaurant. He started the engine and shifted into Reverse, pulling out and then slowing to idle next to her. He rolled the window down. She stopped walking and looked up at him.

"It looks like rain."

"It's a five-minute walk."

He could have shifted back into Drive and gone on, but he didn't. "Where's your car?"

"It wouldn't start this morning, so Katie picked me up."

"I can take a look at it."

She stood there at the side of the road, the wind coming up and whipping her blond hair across her face. She brushed it back and glanced up at the sky. A light mist had started to fall. He'd been guessing about the rain.

"I guess I'll take that ride." She headed around the front of the truck.

He leaned across the seat to open the door for her. "I don't typically predict the weather with that kind of accuracy."

She smiled at that, brushing her hands down rain-dampened arms. It wasn't cold, but in the air-conditioned truck, she probably felt chilled. He reached in the backseat for a jacket and handed it to her.

"Thank you." She wrapped it around her shoulders and pulled her hair free. "Are you as good with cars as you are with the weather?"

"Almost." He glanced her way and saw her hand wipe at her cheeks.

Weather and cars he could handle. Tears were another thing altogether. Especially when those tears were the quiet, stoic kind that made him want to charge to the rescue.

He reminded himself that she'd accepted his offer for a ride, and she was willing to let him look at her car. She hadn't asked to be rescued, and he didn't need to get tangled up in something that would hit a big dead end as soon as she realized she wasn't a small-town girl.

He glanced her way as another tear slid down her cheek. The last thing he wanted to do was get tangled up in something that was temporary. He didn't want to push his way into her life only to find out she wasn't going to stay in Haven.

Those tears were a pretty good—or maybe a pretty bad—sign.

Chapter Five

Macy blamed the rain for the tears slipping unbidden down her cheeks. Just a few drops, easily brushed away. If it hadn't rained, she wouldn't have cried. She would have taken the five-minute walk home, maybe a little melancholy, but she wouldn't have let the tears slip loose.

It wouldn't have been so bad if she hadn't been in Tanner's truck, knowing he had glanced her way and seen her brush the tears away. At least he didn't comment. She was glad for his silence.

What would she have said if he'd asked why she was crying?

It seemed as if, lately, every time it rained, something bad happened. She shook off the thought because it didn't allow for faith. And she had faith. But it had been raining the night the hospital called asking if she was related to Grant Swanson. It had been raining the night Bill broke their engagement. And it had rained the night she'd come to terms with the reality that she couldn't help Colby.

All coincidence, of course. It had been a rainy year in Texas. The news had covered the stories of downpours and floods. So her small story of heartbreak and rainstorms would mean nothing to the outside world.

The truck slowed and drove into the driveway of the craftsman-style home that had belonged to Grant and Cynthia. Tanner pulled next to her car and parked. For a long moment they sat there in silence, neither of them looking at the other. Finally she shrugged out of his jacket and reached for the door handle. Belatedly she grabbed the dessert she'd brought home from the restaurant.

"Thank you for the ride home. I guess it did rain."

In the dark interior of the truck his teeth flashed white in his face. "Just a little. I'll take a look at your car while I'm here."

He was out of the truck before she could tell him it wasn't necessary.

"You don't have to do this," she told him as he headed for her car.

"I don't mind. It's probably something simple. Go ahead and release the hood."

She opened the driver's-side door and pulled

the release. From under the hood she heard him saying something about a hose.

"Go ahead and start it," he called out.

She turned the key, and the car roared to life without a sputter. Tanner pushed the hood down and walked around to join her.

"What was it?"

"Do you always leave your car unlocked?" he asked as she got out, closing the door behind her.

"Sometimes. Why?"

"Someone pulled a hose loose."

"Maybe it just came loose?" She hoped that was the case. It didn't make sense that anyone would tamper with her car. It definitely left her feeling unsettled.

"It didn't just come loose, Macy. Someone un-hooked it. I know Haven is a small town and we like to think we're insulated from real-world problems, but crime does happen here. Make sure you lock the car. And your house."

"I will." She lifted the bag she'd brought from the Candle Light. "Join me for dessert. It isn't much, but since you're standing in the rain fixing my car, I should offer something."

The invitation had slipped out, surprising him. Surprising her.

"I should go," he started. And then he glanced at his watch. "What did you get?"

She grinned at the question. "The giant chocolate turtle cheesecake. It sounded great, and then I couldn't eat it."

"I can't turn down chocolate turtle cheesecake. Do you have coffee?"

"Of course."

"I'm in."

She led him inside, flipping on lights as they went. The house was quiet, but empty without Colby. There were times that it felt like home. But it was still Grant and Cynthia's home. Their furniture, their photographs and their pictures on the walls.

In the kitchen she started the coffee. When she turned, Tanner was pulling plates out of the cabinet.

"You seem to know where to find things better than I do."

He pulled open a drawer and handed her a fork. "I visited a few times. My sister and Cynthia were friends. Grant kept the LSCL informed on school functions and needs in the community that he was aware of through the school."

"I feel like a visitor here," she admitted, and then she was surprised by another round of tears. She brushed away the moisture and turned from his steady, curious gaze. "I'm sorry, I don't know what's wrong with me tonight."

"You lost your brother, your sister-in-law and what was probably a settled life in Dallas."

Not to mention her fiancé. But she was starting to see that as more of a near miss than a loss. If a man wasn't willing to make changes for a child in need, well, she didn't need that man.

"Yes, I suppose. It might feel different if Colby was here, if we were making ourselves into a family. I know that's what Grant wanted, and yet, here I am, and Colby is at the ranch. And the house still feels like their house, like I'm borrowing it. It feels as if they should be coming home any minute, and I'll go back to my life, and Colby will come home and be happy again."

"I'm sorry." He said it softly, and it wasn't a platitude, just a simple acknowledgment of her pain.

"Me, too."

"Make it your own," he countered. "Maybe it's time to pack up what was theirs and make this a home for you and Colby."

"They said to go slow."

"It's been a year. I'm not a therapist, but I think Colby needs to be allowed to move on, too. Maybe it would help him to do this with you. The two of you could go shopping together for new things."

She poured them each a cup of coffee, and he cut the cheesecake into two pieces. They sat down together at the island in the center of the kitchen.

For a few minutes they ate, and she thought about his suggestion. "It might work, you know. If we did this as a team."

"Talk to Bea and to the Macks," he suggested.

"I will."

The cheesecake was chocolate, caramel and pecans. She took a bite and realized Tanner was chuckling. She gave him a sharp look as she slid another bite into her mouth.

"What?" she asked after the next bite.

"It is good, isn't it?"

"Amazing."

His eyes twinkled, and he took another bite of the cake.

"You're still laughing at me," she accused.

He reached for a napkin and turned to face her. "Because you have a little bit of chocolate—" he dabbed at her chin "—right there."

They froze, sitting there facing each other. Her breath caught, the moment taking her by surprise. His hand stilled, and she knew by the way it lingered, by the way his blue eyes darkened to a smoky hue, that he felt it, too.

Slowly he slid from the stool. She looked up, unable to speak her fears, to tell him this was a bad idea. Because in the moment, it felt like the perfect idea. His hand slid to the back of her neck. His other hand cupped her cheek, tilting her head so that when he leaned in, his mouth met hers with ease.

The fork in her left hand dropped on her plate with a clank as she let go and moved her hand to his waist. His lips stilled over hers, but neither of them broke the connection.

Eventually he pulled away, his calloused but gentle hand slid from her neck like a caress, and his lips brushed hers one last time. And she wanted him back, holding her, making her feel safe. A kiss had never made her feel so cherished.

"That wasn't what I'd planned." He said it quietly, and she was glad for that.

She didn't want to be jarred from the moment.

"No, neither had I." She clasped her hands in front of her, afraid they would tremble if left to their own devices.

"I don't want to complicate things," he continued.

She put a finger to her lips. "Then don't say anything, or you will. It was a kiss. And a very nice one. I don't think either of us expected it, but, please, don't say it won't happen again or some other mature and noble thing."

Pushing aside mature, she reached for his hands and gave him a little pull in her direction. Her face tilted toward his was an invitation, and he leaned forward, taking it, dropping another sweet kiss on her lips before pulling away and breaking the connection again.

"I'm not always noble."

She laughed at his words. "I'm glad to hear that."

"But I should go, because this is complicated."

"Hmm," she said, because who could deny the truth? And the second half of that truth was that her heart was still bruised from Bill's rejection.

At least she knew she still had a heart. It could beat wildly and yearn for more than a solitary life.

She walked him to the door. He considered a few dozen ways to apologize, but in the end he decided against what would surely have been a lie. He wasn't at all sorry he'd given her a ride home, and he wasn't sorry he'd kissed her. She was beautiful and kind, and all wrong for him.

He guessed if he was sorry, it was for himself. Because he knew better than to chase something that wasn't meant to be. Sitting in her kitchen, he'd realized just how unsettled she was. She lived in Haven, but it looked as if she might be days away from packing up and leaving.

She wouldn't leave Colby. He'd watched her with her nephew. Maybe she doubted herself, but that little boy didn't doubt her. He just had something buried deep that he needed to work through.

"Good night," he said, standing on her front porch. The rain was coming down in earnest. Somewhere in the distance a siren blasted the quiet of the night.

She reached out, trailing a finger down his cheek. "I wish…"

She shook her head.

He took her hand, kissed her palm and let go. He had to get out of here and get back to the reasonable sanity that usually kept him from making the moonlit night kind of mistakes.

"Good night." She stepped back inside the house.

He took the long way back to his ranch. He drove past the Blue Bonnet Bed and Breakfast. Then he turned and went down Main Street in Haven, past the coffee shop, the library, the grocery store and a few other businesses.

This was his town. He was a part of Haven, and it was part of him. He wouldn't change that for anything. When he thought of the city, he thought of Houston, his parents and chaos. He remembered too well what it had sounded like in that apartment on any given night. The hungry cries of his little sister, the yelling, the fights. And the smell of drugs.

He knew he was biased because of his experiences, but he couldn't undo his past or the way he felt. Cities were just fine. They served a purpose.

As did small towns. This small town had saved his life.

Aunt May. He smiled, remembering a woman who had never married, never had children of her own. But she'd taken in three kids she barely knew, and she'd taken all of their baggage, as well. The fears, the rebellion, the independence.

Travis had been the rebel. Tanner had found trusting a difficult thing to do. He'd kept on doing what he'd done before Aunt May, trying to keep his sister fed, never trusting that Aunt May would have food the next day, or that she'd see to their needs. It had taken trust on his part and patience on hers for them to work past his issues.

He guessed he still hoarded, always fearing that he'd wake up one day and everything would be gone. It was baggage left over from his childhood.

He kept a pantry stocked with food. He kept money in a safe box. He kept to his goals. The list had made sense when he came up with it. College. A career. Buying back the ranch for Aunt May. Savings and a backup plan. And a relationship, someday. The right relationship. A woman who wanted to be a wife and a mom.

One who enjoyed life in a small town and understood ranching.

His brother, Travis, had teased him for that list, telling him he was courting trouble. Trying to keep his life to some kind of schedule only meant the schedule was sure to fall apart. But Tanner had stuck to it, needing the security a plan provided. He maintained his life without entanglements that would drag him back into chaos.

Thirty minutes after leaving Macy, he pulled into the garage of his house. His castle, as Chloe called it. He'd built the house a few years back. It was two-story, stone and stucco, with heavy wood trim. It was open and light, with big windows. Light was important to him.

Open spaces were important.

As he walked through the kitchen and the family room, Chloe appeared. She studied him a little too closely, and then she plopped on the leather sofa and crossed her arms, her head cocked slightly to the side.

"What?" He picked up a book he'd left on the table and pretended he was walking away from her.

She stuck out her leg and stopped him. "Where have you been?"

"Dinner at the Candle Light. We're working

on the people we have to find in order to keep the Culpepper place for the boys."

She stood, going on tiptoe to study his face. And then she reached to wipe his cheek. "Since when does Bea wear that shade of lipstick?"

He rubbed his face, and she laughed.

"Gotcha, big brother. Nothing on your face except a guilty look."

"That's nice," he grumbled. "I'm going to my office."

She grabbed his hand. "Don't go. I'll play nice. I was driving by as you all left the restaurant. I saw Macy Swanson get in your truck."

"You're impossible."

"I'm a little sister. I think impossible is part of the job description. So, she's pretty. And nice. That's a good combination."

"I'm not having this discussion with you."

She sat back down on the sofa. "No, you only want to discuss *my* relationships."

He let it go. He'd learned a long time ago that he wouldn't win if he engaged in an argument with his little sister. "I need to decide which yearlings we're going to put on the website to sell. Do you want to help?"

The question put a smile on her face. "You don't fight fair. Of course I'll accept the distraction and help."

He'd known it would work. Mention horses, and everything else was forgotten.

After raiding the refrigerator, they headed for the computer in his office. Chloe pulled up a chair next to his.

"So, about these people you have to find. Do you want me to help with that?" Chloe asked as he pulled up the inventory of their livestock.

"I might. I'm looking for Gabriel's grandfather Theodore Linley."

"Have you found anything?"

Tanner pulled a few notes out of his desk drawer. "Not much. He hasn't lived around here in years. Gabe doesn't know much about him, other than that he wasn't much of a provider, got into some petty crimes even when he lived around here."

"I hate to ask, but have you checked the prison system?"

No, he hadn't. He let out a long sigh. He didn't want to find his friend's grandfather in a state prison. "I'll take a look."

"You might also check death records."

"Yeah, I will."

"Tanner," she said hesitantly, and he doubted he wanted to hear what came next.

"Yes?" He glanced away from the computer because he knew she'd want his full attention.

"I've been looking for our parents."

"I'm not sure why." He wouldn't even call them parents.

"Because I need to know where they are. I know the word is overused, but I need closure."

He brought up the file of yearling quarter horses. "I understand that."

"Do you know where they are?"

"No, I don't. I haven't tried to find them."

"They visited once, didn't they?"

He leaned back in his chair and allowed the memory he'd been pushing aside for a good many years. "Yes, they came to visit."

"I was four."

"Yes, you were four. And they were..." He shook his head. "Chloe, they were strung out. They wanted money. They weren't here to see their children. They showed up to play on Aunt May's good heart."

"I know, but still. What if they're out there somewhere? Don't you want to know where they are?"

"I don't want to sound coldhearted, Chloe, but you and me, we're coming at this from different places. I remember too much. You don't remember enough."

"But you understand."

That she needed closure? "Yeah, I do."

But that didn't mean he could help her find them. They all had their own version of the past.

His version was about parents who let him down, who left him to be the adult when he'd barely had a chance to be a kid.

She pointed to the file, the conversation about their parents at an end, thankfully. "We had a good crop of foals, didn't we?"

"We did. And I know you hate this part, when we have to let some of them go."

"But that's because we're a working ranch," she mimicked him with a gruff voice. "And if we don't sell our animals, we can't afford to feed them."

"I'm glad you've been listening."

"I've been listening." She moved her chair closer to the computer. "I do want to keep Daisy."

The buttery-yellow filly with a white blaze down a dainty face. "What are you going to do with her?"

"You let me pick one filly a year that I think is special and that will add to our program. She's the one."

"Okay, Daisy is ours." He pointed at the screen, at a light gray colt. "Frosty?"

"He'll grow up to be a good horse for someone."

They worked through the list, and fortunately, the conversation didn't return to their parents. Or to Macy Swanson. Both were topics he wanted to avoid. One was old news.

The other had taken him by surprise.

Chapter Six

Macy showed up at Cabin One on Sunday morning feeling more than a little apprehensive over the pass with Colby. It was the first one they'd had since the failed attempt at a weekend pass. As she walked up the steps, she could hear chaos inside. Someone shouted, and then a loud cry pierced the quiet country morning.

Hand at the ready, she hesitated short of knocking. Before she could make a decision, the door jerked open, and an angry teen stood on the threshold. His eyes widened in shock when he saw her there.

"I'm sorry." His voice was gruff, and he made a move to get past her.

Before he could, Edward Mack was there. The tall redhead was midforties, normally quiet and always concerned with the boys at the ranch.

"Johnny, when we're talking, you're not to walk out that door."

Macy took a step back, unsure of her next move. Should she go inside and collect Colby or step aside and wait out whatever was taking place? Edward answered her unspoken question.

"Macy, Colby is in his room. Give us a few minutes, and we'll allow them all out." Edward had a hand on Johnny Drake's back. "Johnny, let's take a walk."

Edward and the boy stepped out the door, and Macy moved aside to let them pass. From inside she heard Eleanor call out, telling her to go ahead and come in. Macy walked through the cabin and found Eleanor in the hall.

"I think I came at a bad time."

Eleanor waved off the apology. "No, it's okay. Johnny has been doing so well, but he still has his moments. He and Ben had a disagreement. We put the boys in their rooms until we know the episode is over, and everything and everyone is safe again."

"They're all okay, though?"

"Yes, they're fine. They're unfortunately used to this. They go to their rooms, play with toys, color or read. When the crisis is over, we give the all clear. Which I think is right now." Eleanor cleared her throat. "Boys, come on out."

Two doors opened. Ben peeked his head out and looked down the hall. "He's not waiting for me?"

"No," Eleanor assured him. "He's outside with Edward. But I'm sure we'll all sit down and talk."

The other door opened. Colby stepped out and, behind him, eleven-year-old Sam Clark with his pale blond hair and serious blue eyes.

"Aunt Macy!" Colby rushed forward and wrapped thin arms around her waist. Macy pulled him close, her heart taken by surprise at the greeting.

"Hey, sweetie, you ready for church?"

He nodded against her stomach. As she slipped past, Eleanor patted Macy's shoulder. "You two have a good day. Be back by five this afternoon."

"We can do that." She separated from her nephew. "Is there anything you need to get?"

He hurried back into his room for a backpack and came out with it slung over his shoulder. "I'm ready to go. See you later, Sam."

Sam stood in the door to the room they shared, solemn and worried. "You'll be okay, Colby?"

"Yeah, I'll be okay," her nephew reassured the other boy, and then he took her hand and led her from the cabin.

The weather was perfect for the first part of October. It was still warm, but with less humidity and a light breeze that made it ideal for the time of year. And with Colby holding her hand and talking a mile a minute about a new cow he'd fed and the big move, it was easy to believe everything would be okay.

They arrived at church as the bell was ringing, and people were hurrying inside. Macy parked, and she and Colby ran together, the backpack swinging at his side. Chloe Barstow was entering just ahead of them. The younger woman held the door.

"I'm late, too. We had a mare foaling. I didn't want to leave her," Chloe explained. She ruffled her hand through Colby's hair. "Hey, Colby, good to see you."

Colby grinned at the other woman. He'd been raised in this church. His parents had taken an active role, working with the youth. Like the house, the church had been theirs. Macy often felt like a placeholder. She could handle that at church, even in the house, but she wanted to be so much more to Colby.

"Can I sit with the Wayes?" Colby asked as they entered the sanctuary and looked for a place to land.

The Waye family had been Grant and Cynthia's closest friends. And it was easy to see Colby's connection with them. It was easy to see that Laurie Waye, the mother, had natural instincts.

Macy envied her that gift.

"Of course you can," she answered when she

realized her nephew still stood waiting for her to respond.

He skipped away, leaving her to find a seat alone. A hand touched her elbow. Chloe Barstow nodded toward a few empty seats. "Sit with me? Tanner is at home with the mare and new foal. He probably won't be here."

"Thank you," Macy whispered, following the other woman to the empty spots.

"No problem."

They sat and the music started. Chloe touched her arm.

"Colby loves you," she said in hushed tones. "I know you worry, but don't."

"It's hard not to." She tried to focus on the music, but her gaze kept straying to her young nephew. He seemed so happy with the Waye family. There was a mom, a dad and several children. A real family. A dad to play basketball. The kind of mom who knew how to bake cookies without burning them. They probably had a strong extended family with grandparents, aunts, uncles and cousins.

Macy had no one, really. Her dad had passed away years ago. Her mom, Nora, lived in Arizona. She'd come to Texas following the accident and then the funeral. But then her husband, Macy's stepfather, had called and asked her to come home. And she'd gone. For a few weeks after she'd gone back to Arizona, they'd talked on the phone every day. Now they talked once a week. Every Sunday at seven.

"I know it will get easier. Just give it time," Chloe offered.

Of course, she nodded, because she had to believe that things would get better.

Again her attention focused on the Wayes. A real family. Maybe that was what Colby needed? And it was something she couldn't give him. It was just the two of them. She closed her eyes, praying away the pain and wishing God would give her a clear sign.

What if she wasn't meant to raise Colby? What if someone else could do this and make him happy? She shuddered, thinking about letting go. It hurt too much to even contemplate. But could she do it if it was the best thing for her nephew?

"You okay?"

The service was ending. She gathered up her Bible and purse. "Yes, I'm good."

Chloe opened her mouth to respond, but Colby raced back to them, a coloring page in his hand. "I colored this for you."

She took the page and held it up to study the image of Jesus calming the storm. *Why are you afraid?* it said in bold letters at the top of the page.

"Well, I guess that's a direct message," Chloe said with a hint of laughter. "Hey, why don't the two of you join us for lunch at the castle? I mean, the ranch."

"Castle?" Colby perked up.

"That's what she calls my place," Tanner said, appearing at Macy's side. "It's actually my kingdom. Sometimes she forgets."

"You have a kingdom?" Colby, still amazed by the castle, now had a kingdom to imagine.

Chloe nodded. "He does. And he's the king. But I thought he was at home taking care of horses."

The last sentence was obviously directed at her brother, and Chloe gave him a look to let him know.

He shrugged. "The new foal is doing great. I slipped in after the service started. And if Macy and Colby want to join us for lunch, that's fine with me."

"We shouldn't," Macy started. Chloe cut her off.

"If you have other plans, that's okay. But it's just the two of us and a big roast in the slow cooker. Someone should help us eat it. And we might need help naming that new foal."

Macy caught a look between brother and sister. She started to give excuses why she and Colby couldn't join them, but Colby grabbed her hand.

"Could we go?"

Tanner smiled down at her nephew. And then he raised his gaze to meet hers. Something in his dark blue eyes unsettled her.

"You should join us. If you don't, we'll be eating roast all week." Tanner touched a hand to Colby's shoulder.

That settled it for her. Colby needed people. He needed men who would be role models and do things with him that a father would have done. She could toss a ball, she could teach him to drive, but he needed male role models in his life.

"We'd love to join you all. Is there anything I can bring?"

"No, we have everything," Chloe responded. "You can follow us."

Colby could barely contain himself. As they followed the dark blue Ford truck in the direction of the Barstow ranch, her nephew talked nonstop about castles and kingdoms. She gave up trying to convince him that they were just going to a regular house. He wanted to believe that they were on their way to Tanner Barstow's kingdom and that the rancher was some sort of king. Or worse, that he was a knight in shining armor.

Macy tried to picture that knight with a cowboy hat. She smiled at the thought, until she remembered the way he'd held her just days earlier.

She might need a rescuer, but she thought it

more likely she needed someone to rescue her heart from memories of a kiss.

Tanner turned up his drive and shot Chloe a look that she happily ignored. She saw, but she shifted away and pretended she didn't. Instead she sang along to a George Strait song and dug through her purse for a piece of gum.

"What are you up to?" he finally asked.

She looked up, a flash of guilt quickly dissolving into an innocent smile. "Up to?"

"Inviting Macy to lunch?" He let that thought ruminate for a few seconds. "Did you put that book in her bag?"

"Book?"

No, of course she didn't. Now he was getting paranoid. "Macy has a lot on her plate. The last thing she needs is you trying to involve yourself in her life."

Anger flashed in his sister's blue eyes. "Really? Did it ever cross your mind that I might like Macy? She's new in town, and she's had a tough year. She needs friends. So does Colby. If it feels like I'm trying to manipulate your life, maybe you should think how I feel."

"Touché," he said. "I'm sorry."

"You should be. And would it hurt you to take a look at a really nice woman?"

"I've looked," he admitted.

That made his sister happy. "Well, isn't that surprising. And?"

"I'm busy, Chloe. Yes, I want to get married and have a family." Lately, he'd thought about it a lot. A wife. Kids. It was what he'd always wanted. "I don't want to get involved in a relationship with someone who might not stay in Haven."

Her eyes widened. "Why don't you think she'll stay? She has Colby, and this is his home."

"Several reasons," he said, and he had to make it quick because he was pulling into the garage. "She's from Dallas. I learned something in plant sciences and that's that a plant doesn't do well when taken from its native surroundings. She's all city. I can't see her lasting in our small town. And second, Colby has a lot of memories here. It could be that a fresh start elsewhere would help him to move on."

"I hadn't thought of that. But would it be good to take him from what he's always known?"

"Sometimes a fresh start helps."

"Sometimes you have to give people a chance," she countered as she got out of the truck. "You could at least play nice."

He shook his head as he got out to follow her inside. Yeah, he could play nice. As a matter of fact, he'd tried, and he'd actually enjoyed it. It didn't take much to remember the way it had felt to hold Macy. He could imagine the scent of her hair, the way it had felt to kiss her, the way her hands had touched his face.

He hadn't been prepared for the attraction. And it went beyond attraction. He liked her. Liking her added a whole other level of complication.

"She's the mother of a resident at the ranch," he grumbled at his sister's retreating back. "That changes things."

She glanced back at him, a frown in place. "She won't always be the mom of a resident. Colby will go home. And I think Macy will stay and make Haven her home.

"I'll go let them in," she offered. "Do you want to turn the oven on so I can heat the rolls?"

Anything to stay busy.

He was pouring tea in glasses when Macy, Colby and Chloe joined him. Colby was wide-eyed as he look around the kitchen and up at the high ceilings.

"Wow. It is a castle."

"Colby," Macy cautioned. "Why don't you wash your hands? And is there something I can do to help?"

"You can put the glasses on the table," Tanner suggested. But he wished he hadn't. He should have told her to go ahead and sit down. That would have put her a good thirty feet from him and out of reach. But instead she was next to him, her arm brushing his as she grabbed a couple of glasses. And he couldn't help but lean a little in her direction. That shift brought him close enough that he caught the herbal scent of her shampoo.

She didn't notice, but across the room Chloe did. A wink told him she'd caught the move.

Colby finished washing his hands and hurried past them, nearly bumping into his aunt. Tanner caught the boy up in his arms. "Slow down, buddy, or you'll take someone down."

The kid grinned, but he nodded affably. "Okay. But after we eat, can I see that new horse?"

"Yeah, you can see the new horse."

"Is it a black stallion?"

"Yes, and when I ride it, I'm going to wear armor and carry a sword."

Colby laughed. "You're not really a knight because my aunt says this isn't a castle. It's a really big house. Too big for two people."

The aunt in question was on her way to the dining room with glasses of tea, but he heard her gasp. She turned, her cheeks faintly pink. "Colby."

Tanner considered rescuing her but decided against it.

Chloe jumped in. "It is too big for two people,

Colby. That's why Tanner needs to get married and have a bunch of kids."

He should have known.

"He could let kids from the ranch live here with him," Colby suggested.

"That's a great idea," Chloe continued. "Tanner, why don't you do that?"

"I'm going to get the roast." Tanner turned tail and ran. He'd never considered himself a coward, but any man would be if he had to face his sister. Add Colby and the pink-faced Macy, and he was outnumbered.

He was a man who liked goals, and today's goal was clear. Finish this meal as quickly as possible, before Chloe could take meddling to a whole new level.

Chapter Seven

Monday, after a long day substituting for the high school algebra teacher, Macy headed for the Silver Star. She had a bag with treats for the boys and the book that someone thought she should read. It no longer mattered who had left the book in her book bag. What mattered was that it would give her time with Colby. The other boys would enjoy it, too.

She pulled up to the ranch house, waving to Flint as he headed out to the barn with a few of the older boys. As she walked toward the house, a loud explosion shook the air. From a distance she heard screams. The horses in the field took off at a dead run. Heart pounding, Macy ran for the cabin where Colby would be with the Macks.

Edward Mack was running in that direction, too. They met on the steps, and she followed him inside.

"What was that?" she asked as they hurried through the door.

Edward closed the door behind her and locked it. "I'm not sure. But we aren't taking any chances."

Eleanor was in the living room with Colby, Sam and Ben. "What was that?"

Edward shook his head. "Where's Johnny?"

The fifteen-year-old with the quiet demeanor, curly brown hair and easy smile was missing. Eleanor had an arm around Colby and Sam, the two taking comfort in her strong presence. Macy stood there, not knowing what she should do. She had known only that, when she'd heard that explosion, Colby was somewhere, and she needed to make sure he was safe.

"Johnny is with Doc Harrow. They're working with sick calves."

"You all stay here. I'm going to see what I can find out." Edward headed for the door. Macy followed, locking the door behind him.

"So, what will we do, boys?" Eleanor asked with a smile that was probably meant to tell them everything was okay.

"I have a book I planned on reading," Macy offered. "Unless you have something else?"

"A story is a great idea. Boys, what do you think?"

Colby and Sam nodded and moved from her side. Ben looked unsure.

"Ben, it's up to you," Eleanor told him.

"I'll stay with Miss Macy," he said quietly, a little unsure. He was in his early teens but still a boy. Macy motioned him toward the furniture, a big sectional and two recliners that filled the small room.

"I like this story," Colby said. "It's one of my favorites."

Macy sat down, Sam and Colby on either side of her and Ben in one of the recliners. It gave her pause that the mystery person had left one of Colby's favorite books for her to read.

The front door unlocked as she started to read. Edward stepped in with a few more of the younger boys and the house mom from Cabin Three, Laura Davidson. She was in her fifties, and she and her husband had been at the ranch for quite a few years. They'd never had children of their own, but she loved the ranch kids as if they were hers.

"Laura and the boys are going to join you all for story time," Edward informed her, and then he was gone again.

Laura herded in her boys. "Morgan, Billy and Jasper, do you all know Miss Macy?"

The little boy she knew as Jasper stepped forward, his sandy-colored hair a mess and his eyes twinkling with orneriness. "Yes, ma'am. She told us a dragon story."

"Okay, let's have a seat, and I'll go see if Eleanor needs any help."

Jasper gave her a sweet smile and sat down on the floor. She knew the little boy from the library and wouldn't doubt if he had superglue hidden somewhere on his person. He'd glued a book to her desk a few weeks ago.

"Is Colby going home with you?" Morgan Duff asked as she opened the book. He looked up at her so seriously, his brown eyes luminous behind his glasses.

"Of course he is," she replied. And then she wondered if that was the right answer. Morgan looked away, his hands clasping at his side.

"Morgan, are you okay?" She leaned toward him, and he looked up.

"Yeah. I hope he does go home. He's just a kid."

Her heart broke a little on those words. Morgan was about ten, and a child himself. He was someone's broken little boy with anger issues and a hurting heart.

"You're a good friend to worry about him," she told Morgan.

"We're more like family than friends," he said.

"Yes, definitely."

Jasper groaned. "Could we read now?"

"Yes, we can read."

She started the story, and the boys moved

closer, even Ben, who pretended to be too old for stories. She wondered about the teenager. He was quiet and respectful, always looking out for the younger boys. And yet he was here at the ranch. Someone had mentioned parents on drugs.

Each child had a story. And they had the ranch to help them change their stories for the better.

She was on page twenty when Eleanor stepped back into the room. "I have cookies and hot cocoa if anyone is interested."

The boys jumped up and hurried from the room. All but Colby. He remained at her side on the sofa, his head tucked against her shoulder.

"What do you think made that noise, Aunt Macy?" His voice was small and worried.

"I think probably a car backfiring." Or she would like to believe that was the cause.

"What's a backfire?"

"Hmm, good question. I guess I don't know what causes a backfire. I can look it up, and then we'll both learn something new. But it happens sometimes. A car will be driving and suddenly make a loud sound."

"Oh. I've heard that before. My dad..." His voice trailed off.

Macy held her breath, waiting. He almost never mentioned his parents.

"Colby, it's okay to talk about them."

He shook his head. "I'm mad at them."

The response took the air from her lungs and made her heart ache. She wanted to tell him that was wrong. Instead she asked, "Why?"

He shrugged slim shoulders and pulled away from the arm she'd put around him. "They shouldn't have left."

"No," she agreed. "They shouldn't have left. But they didn't have a choice."

"Yes, they did. They didn't have to go out. They didn't have to leave me."

Tears were streaming down his cheeks. He curled into a ball on the sofa. Macy touched his shoulder and tried to pull him close. He stiffened and wouldn't budge.

Eleanor appeared at her side. She briefly touched Macy's shoulder, and then she got down on her knees at Colby's side and put a hand on his back.

"Care to talk, Colby?"

He shook his head. "I don't want to talk. Talking hurts."

"Yes, but sometimes it hurts and then makes it better. Did you ever cut your finger, Colby, and just when you thought it was getting better, it started to hurt and itch?"

He nodded.

"That's when it's healing. It hurts, but it's getting better. Your parents didn't know that, when they left, they weren't coming back. Do you think if they'd known, they would have left? I think they would have stayed home with you."

He shook his head and wouldn't look up.

"Do you have a reason to think they wanted to go?"

He nodded, but he wouldn't talk.

Eleanor brushed a hand across the top of his head. "Do you want your aunt Macy to hold you? Sometimes when I'm sad, it helps if I get a hug."

Without a word he turned and crawled into Macy's lap. And he cried. She tucked his head under her chin and allowed her own silent tears to fall.

Eleanor grabbed a few tissues out of the box on the end table and handed them to her, and then she left them alone. Macy cradled her nephew in her arms and told him everything would be okay. She hoped he believed it, because sometimes she wondered.

Edward unlocked the door to Cabin One, and Tanner followed him inside. He knew the kids were safe, and with Eleanor and Laura on the job, the kids were probably seeing this as a great adventure and nothing to worry about. He didn't expect to see Macy on the sofa cradling Colby in her arms as the little boy cried.

He also didn't expect the crazy urge to go to them and make their problems his. As a matter of fact, when Edward kept moving, giving them privacy, Tanner told himself to keep on moving, too.

For the first time in a long time, he didn't listen to his better self. Nope, he headed right into the situation, settling himself in a recliner that had been pulled close to the sectional. Macy looked up, her green eyes swimming with tears.

"Hey, Colby," he said quietly.

"Hey, Tanner," the little boy said in a tearful voice.

"Bad day?" Tanner guessed that was an understatement.

Colby nodded against his aunt's shoulder. "I miss my..."

But he wouldn't say it. He never did. Not a mention of his mom or his dad. Tanner had noticed. He'd heard other people comment on it.

"You miss your mom and dad?" Tanner prodded. He wasn't a therapist, but he knew all about being a kid and wanting his parents.

In his case he'd wanted his parents to actually *be* parents. And he'd even kind of hoped that once the state took custody and placed them with Aunt May, that their parents would get their act together.

He'd taken a few classes and even gone through foster parent training because he wanted to know the laws and the emotions of the kids at the ranch. He knew that, no matter how bad a home situation might have been, kids always wanted their biological parents. Colby hadn't been taken from abusive parents. He'd had his parents taken from him.

"Yeah," Colby finally answered. "I miss them."

"That's okay, you know."

Colby nodded and pulled away from Macy to sit up. He wiped his face with his hand, and Macy handed him a tissue.

"How's your new horse?" Colby asked, done with the tears.

"He's real good. One of these days, your aunt Macy can bring you out to see him again." He'd shown Colby the horse the previous day, after they'd finished lunch.

Colby looked up at her. "Today?"

Tanner laughed. "I think we're going to be kind of busy today."

"Because a car backfired?" Colby asked, sniffling and brushing his hand across his eyes.

Tanner looked at Macy, and she arched a brow and gave him a well-meaning look. Okay, backfiring cars. Why not?

"Yeah, because of that."

Macy gave Colby a hug. "How about cookies and cocoa now?"

Colby slid off her lap and headed for the kitchen. Tanner didn't know what to do after the boy left and it was just him and Macy in the living room. She looked about to fall apart. He wasn't sure what he'd do if she picked his shoulder for that event.

But she didn't fall apart. Instead she took a deep breath.

"I want to fix him," she said in a quiet voice, her gaze on the door her nephew had gone through.

"Of course you do. It takes time. But he's turning to you. That's new, isn't it?"

"Yes, it is. I can't describe how it felt when he crawled onto my lap and let me hold him. He doesn't often do that."

"That's a starting place." He stood, needing space. "The police are on their way. Tell Edward I'll be at the barn waiting."

"What happened?"

"Someone shot a hole in the barn. Fortunately it lodged in a support pole."

Her face paled. "I was hoping it was just…"

He grinned. "A car backfiring?"

"Yeah."

"I wish it had been." He glanced at his watch. "And Chloe's fiancé is going to be here in an hour. He's going to volunteer. It's a chance for me to get to know him."

"Chloe seems to love him."

Tanner brushed his fingers through his hair,

surprised by this conversation. "Yeah, she seems to. Bring Colby by when you can to see Knight again."

"Knight?" Her voice had a teasing quality to it.

"A castle needs one, don't you think?"

"Yes, I guess it would."

He left. As he headed for the barn, Gabriel Everett was pulling up. Behind him were county police. And Fletcher. Great.

Gabriel was out of his truck first. "What happened out here?"

Beatrice came out of the barn, her eyebrows drawn together in worry. "We were shot at, that's what. And keep it down, Gabriel. We don't want to scare the boys."

Fletcher was upon them. "And how do we know it wasn't one of your boys, Bea? I keep telling you all that this is getting out of hand. Fifty years ago, troubled boys were a lot less dangerous. We live in different times. These boys have different problems. And we don't need those problems in our community."

"Fletcher, this is a level one facility. We don't take boys with serious behavioral problems, and you know that."

"Bea, I think you take any kid that the state brings you."

"Maybe I do, Fletcher, but the state also knows what we're equipped to handle. We don't have the facilities for truly troubled youth, and so the state takes those boys to placements that can handle them."

Fletcher shook his head. "We need to have a meeting and discuss this."

Gabriel stepped forward. "Fletcher, the last time I checked, you weren't a member of the LSCL, and so you don't get to call meetings. I'm the president. I call meetings."

"Then call one," Fletcher said. "Call one, or I'll call the state and find out what we can do to close this place down."

"Don't threaten this place." Gabriel issued the warning in a stern voice that no one should ignore.

Fletcher ignored it. "I'm not threatening…"

Tanner held up a hand. "Please, don't say it was a promise, not a threat. Because if you do, I'm going to laugh."

Bea chuckled. The moment slid into a less hostile one. The deputies were out of their cars and taking notes. Tanner stepped back, not wanting to get in their way. Fletcher, on the other hand, was in the middle of everything.

Gabriel stepped close to Tanner. "This is getting out of hand with him."

"I know. I'm just not sure what to do about it. I think once we get to the Culpepper place, he'll have to stop because it won't have anything to do with him."

Gabriel adjusted his black Stetson. "I'm afraid he'll fight us legally and try to close the ranch."

"We'll fight back. We can outspend him."

"True, but…" Gabriel started but let his words trail off.

"Gabriel, don't tell me you're rethinking the ranch."

"No, I'm not. I'm just worried. What if a boy had been in the path of that bullet?"

The reality of that settled over Tanner, turning him cold.

"I'd rather not think about that." Because thinking about it brought an image of Colby Swanson for some reason.

Tanner cared about the kids at the ranch. All of them. He saw himself in each of them. Colby was different. Maybe knowing Macy made the difference in how he felt about the boy.

"Someone is going to get hurt," Gabriel continued.

"Then we have to find who did this."

"Yeah, I hope we can."

Tanner heard a door. He looked back and saw Macy leaving Cabin One. He let out a sigh and shook his head.

"If you feel like you need to stop her, go." Gabriel jerked his head in Macy's direction.

"I don't." Tanner shot another look her way. "I wanted to see if the two of us could sit down to discuss your grandfather. I know this is bad timing, Gabe. I know you've got reasons you don't want to discuss him. But we have a dozen kids moving at the end of the month, and I sure don't want to take a chance that we might have to move them back over here."

"We can talk. After the meeting at the end of the week."

"That works." He glanced back over his shoulder again.

"Go."

Tanner stood there a full minute, watching the officers, watching Bea soothe Fletcher's ruffled feathers, and then he walked away.

When he caught up with Macy, she was standing in the yard of the cabin, her back to him.

"We have a shooter on the loose, no idea who it is and where they are, and you're standing out here in the yard." He jerked off his hat and looked around.

That was when he noticed the slight tremble in her shoulders. He shoved his hat back on his head and reached, letting his hand hover above her shoulder for a second before allowing it to settle. She turned, and he lost the battle to remain detached.

But he also wasn't going to stand in the yard

and be the next target. He took her by the hand and led her at a fast walk toward his truck. Tears were streaming down her cheeks, her eyes were puffy and her nose was red. A woman in crisis. She wasn't his problem, he reminded himself on the short trek to his truck.

For the life of him, he couldn't walk away from her. Even when he reminded himself that he didn't get involved with parents who had boys at the ranch.

He opened the door of his truck and motioned her inside. Once she was in and buckled, he drove away.

"I'm sorry," she said softly with a hint of a sob.

"What happened?" And with that question he knew he was digging a deeper hole.

"Nothing." She shook her head. "Not really. It's just a roller coaster. And I want to fix this all for him, and I can't. I'm mad at my brother, too. But I don't get to be angry because I have to find a way to help Colby get past his grief and his anger."

"You have a right to be angry."

"I also have a car back at the ranch."

He chuckled. "You can get it later."

She leaned back in the seat and covered her face with her hands. A growl, muffled by her hands, split the silence of the truck. "I am angry.

I'm so mad at him for leaving. I'm mad because I don't know what to do for Colby. And the person I always went to for advice is gone. Grant is gone. I think Colby and I were both in a delusional state, thinking they would come home. But they're not coming home. I'm not getting my brother, my best friend, back. Colby isn't getting his parents back. They're just gone. And it isn't fair. It isn't fair that I had to—"

Her eyes closed, and she shook her head.

"Macy?"

She pinched the bridge of her nose. "No. I'm not going to say that. I lost a job and gave up an apartment. Colby lost his parents. What I lost doesn't amount to anything. I lost things I don't miss."

"I think you're wrong. I think you miss your life. There's nothing wrong with that. Accept it, or it'll eat you up."

He pulled up to her house.

"I miss my life." She said it on a sigh. "I wouldn't be anywhere else. But I have to admit, there are days I wonder if Colby would be better off with someone else, with anyone but me. But I'm his family. We have each other."

"Yes, and in the end, that matters."

"But…" She bit down on her lip and glanced away from him, not finishing.

"But what?"

"What if I'm not a mom? What if I can't do this?" She looked young sitting next to him, her green eyes troubled. "I'm sorry, you didn't ask for this, to be the person I pour out my insecurities on. I lost the person I always went to when I was upset. I don't know how to do this, and Grant isn't here for me to talk to. If he was, I'd tell him I'm not sure if I know how to be a mom. And what if I hurt Colby in the process of learning?"

"I think that anyone would question their ability. I'm guessing that even a mom who planned on having a child would still question if she could do it."

She reached for the door. "Thank you. I'm sorry that you had to leave when there were probably things you needed to do."

He raised a hand to stop her apology. "No trouble. If I'd stayed, I might have been arrested for hurting Fletcher."

He got out and walked her to the front door.

"I would have bailed you out," she said with a hint of a smile. "If you'd punched him. Oh, what about my car?"

"I'll have Flint help me get it over here."

The car reminded him. She'd been vandalized. He couldn't help but wonder if the person who had disconnected that hose on her car was the same person who had shot at the barn. When he got back to the ranch, he would mention that to the police.

"Macy, you need to be careful. Just keep an eye on things around here. Keep your car locked."

"I will. Thank you for letting me talk about Colby."

"Anytime." He said it, and then he realized the door that had opened.

She laughed. "Don't worry. I won't be calling at midnight to talk about my feelings."

"If you did, I'd answer."

She stood on tiptoe and touched his cheek to bring it down to her level. When she kissed him, he felt floored by the unexpected gesture.

He also felt like a man wading into quicksand, because he wasn't satisfied with that sweet kiss on the cheek. Standing on her porch in broad daylight, he turned and brushed his lips against hers.

"See you later," he said as he stepped back to leave.

"Yes, later."

He drove away thinking about that old saying "Out of the frying pan and into the fire." This was one of those situations, he realized.

Macy had soft hair, soft gestures and a soft

heart. She was easy to like. He guessed if a man wasn't careful, he'd find himself falling a little in love with her.

Chapter Eight

Macy pulled up in front of Lila's Café on Tuesday morning. She was meeting Josie Markham for breakfast before she headed out to the ranch for family therapy with Colby. Since she was early, she walked down the sidewalk and stopped in front of the secondhand shop. The store had a cute selection of shabby chic furniture. Old dressers, desks, chairs and tables that were painted light colors.

Maybe, she thought, she could purchase a few pieces to lighten up the darker colors in Grant's house. No, not Grant and Cynthia's house, her house.

"Hey, that's a long sigh for such a pretty day."

She turned, managing a smile for Josie. "It is a pretty day. I'm window-shopping."

"We should go in."

"No, I don't think so. Moving forward isn't easy, is it?"

The humor in Josie's eyes dimmed. "No, it isn't. What does that have to do with furniture?"

"It isn't my house. It's my brother's house. He and his wife decorated it."

"And you haven't made it your own?"

They were walking toward the café. "No, I haven't. It feels as if they will walk in any moment, so it would be wrong to change their home. It feels wrong to move into their home, their lives and their shoes."

"And that's something I can understand. Moving on is difficult."

They entered the café that was less than crowded. They'd purposely missed the morning rush. The waitress, a young woman with a bouncy ponytail and braces, hurried forward to take their order.

"I'll take coffee and a cinnamon roll." Josie turned her coffee cup for the girl to fill it.

"I'll have the same."

Macy waited until the waitress left. "I'm so sorry, Josie. I get so caught up in my life. How are you doing?"

Josie shrugged a slim shoulder. "Some days better than others. Today is a good day. I can talk about it today. I can think about the baby and being a mom, and I don't feel as if my whole life is a nightmare that I can't wake up from. And today I'm trusting God instead of being angry with Him."

"Have you picked a name?"

Josie grinned and wagged a finger. "No, and I'm not telling."

"I'll get it out of you yet."

The door opened. Macy looked up, surprised to see Fletcher Snowden Phillips walking in. He shot her a look, shook his head and headed for the front counter, where the waitress was bagging up a to-go order. She didn't have a clue why he'd be upset with her. And really, she didn't care. Fletcher seemed to have a lot of his own baggage to deal with.

"He's called a meeting of the LSCL," Josie informed her, pausing as the waitress returned with their breakfast. She waited until the girl left to continue. "I heard Gabriel Everett wasn't happy about it and told him he didn't have the right to call meetings. But Fletcher is determined. He says the Silver Star has become something other than what it started out to be, and he won't have it being a blight on the community."

"I can't imagine someone knowing that place the way he does and still believing it should be shut down."

"He's always been against it. For as long as

I can remember, he has disliked the ranch and the boys."

"I don't know what Colby and I would have done without the ranch."

"How is Colby?"

Macy pulled the cinnamon roll apart with her fork. "I'm not really sure. Some days I think we'll make it. And then there are days that I'm positive I'm doing the wrong thing for him. There are days I just know that he needs more than I can give."

"More?"

"A real family," she admitted. "I don't know the first thing about being a mother. So how could I be mom and dad to a little boy?"

Josie touched her belly. "And do you think I do? Parenting is on-the-job training. And you already have the most important part. You love him."

"Yes, I do. And I am already at a place where I don't know what I'd do without him."

"Then give it time," Josie encouraged.

On his way out Fletcher stopped at their table. "Good morning, ladies."

"Fletcher," Josie responded. "You know Macy. Her nephew is at the ranch."

Fletcher gave her a long, steady look. "I'm not sure that's the safest place for a young child."

"I believe it is," she responded. "It's been a great place for him."

"Aren't you also on the LSCL committee to help find the missing members of the ranch?" Fletcher asked.

Macy looked up at him, a bite of cinnamon roll on her fork. "Yes, Mr. Phillips, I am. And I intend to find them and make sure the boys get that bigger ranch."

"You will have your work cut out for you." He inclined his head.

Fletcher left, and Macy shuddered as he walked out the door. Josie's eyes were big, and her lips twitched with a suppressed smile.

Macy's phone rang, and she reached into her purse for it. The number was out of state. She answered.

"Hello, my name is Avery Culpepper. I received a message from Macy Swanson," the chipper voice on the other end announced.

Macy set her fork down. "I'm Macy Swanson. And I left that message, Miss Culpepper."

"Yeah, well, you found me. Old Cyrus was my grandfather. I didn't know him, though. My dad left years ago."

"I see. Mr. Culpepper was very interested in finding you." She hesitated, unsure of how to proceed because part of this message would include telling this young woman that her grandfather was deceased.

"Was interested? Did he give up?" Avery Culpepper had a jarring voice. Macy told herself it was just the phone.

"No, he didn't give up. He passed away, and it was in his will that we should try to find you."

"Did he leave me something? He had a ranch, didn't he?" The voice was definitely jarring. No blaming the phone for that tone.

"Yes, he did own a ranch. Miss Culpepper, I really can't go into this on the phone, and it isn't my place to give specifics. I was just asked to find you."

"Right, okay, well, I'm kind of tied up right now. It might take me a week or so to get there. Haven, right?"

"Yes, right outside Waco. But there's really no need for you to come here yet. March is when everything will be settled. Let me give you the name of the lawyer so you can touch base and he can tell you what you need to do." Macy sent a grimace in Josie's direction because the other woman looked too hopeful, too excited.

"Yeah, well, I'll be there as soon as I get some business taken care of."

"But there's no need for you to—"

The call ended. Macy looked at the phone, amazed.

"Well, was it her?" Josie asked.

"I guess it was."

Josie's smile disappeared. "What's wrong?"

She shrugged, "Nothing. She was just very… harsh?"

"Maybe she'll be better in person. And we don't have to like her. We just have to find her," Josie reminded her.

"That's true."

They were finishing their cinnamon rolls when the front door opened. Macy's heart stuttered a little when Tanner walked in, taking off his hat as he approached their table.

"Tanner, how are you this morning?" Josie shot Macy a questioning look before she offered the greeting.

"Good, Josie. How are you doing?" He reached for a chair and pulled it to their table.

Macy was glad when he sat down. Craning her neck to look up at him hadn't been comfortable. As he sat down, he turned his attention on her.

"We're having a meeting of the LSCL to address Fletcher's *concerns*. We're also going to discuss our search."

"Oh, I just got off the phone a few minutes ago. With Avery Culpepper."

"That's about the best news I've had today. The way this has been going, I wondered if Cyrus just wanted to mess with us all."

"I think we've all been feeling that way."

He stood again. "I'm going to meet early with Gabe. If you could be at his place in thirty minutes, we're gathering in his library."

"I can be there."

"Good." He inclined his head. "Josie, if you need anything…"

"Thanks, Tanner." Josie smiled at him as he left, and then her inquiring gaze landed on Macy, her eyebrow arched; she tapped her fingers on the table.

"What?"

Josie stopped tapping. "That was interesting."

"Interesting?"

"Macy, Tanner is a nice guy, but he doesn't typically come in and sit down. He issues orders and moves on."

Macy could have agreed. That had been the Tanner she'd first met when she came to Haven. He'd been busy. He'd rushed in the day she arrived, telling her he was sorry, asking if she needed anything. He'd left a casserole on his way out the door and a card with his business number.

This new Tanner was an enigma. And she liked him.

"You're quiet," Josie said.

"I'm sorry." Macy shook her head. "I was thinking."

"About Tanner Barstow, no doubt." Josie wiped sticky fingers with a napkin. "Chloe says he wants nothing more than to get married and have a bunch of kids. He's been so focused on building the ranch and his business, she thinks he's kind of gotten sidetracked."

"I really like Chloe, but I doubt Tanner wants her sharing his life with everyone in town," Macy answered. At Josie's widened eyes she realized she'd messed up. "I'm sorry. I'm just being overly sensitive. I'm worried about Colby, the ranch and what I'm going to do to make things right. And Tanner is…" What was Tanner?

"A distraction?" Josie replied, unrepentant, it seemed. "A very gorgeous and super wealthy distraction."

Macy shook her head at her friend's tenaciousness. "Yes, he is that. And I think I've already proved that I can't be on a list of 'wife and mother' candidates. I can't even manage to make one little boy happy."

"Don't be so hard on yourself."

"Tell that to my heart," Macy replied, glancing at the clock on her phone. "I should get to that meeting. A rain check on shopping?"

"Deal. But do me a favor. Give yourself a chance. And give Colby a chance."

Macy gave her friend a quick hug, and then she hurried out the door. She had twenty minutes to get to the meeting. Twenty minutes to prepare herself to face Tanner. She'd kissed him. She'd taken the first step. She'd never been that person. Not once in her life had she been the initiator in a relationship.

But it had seemed so natural to stand on tiptoe and kiss his cheek. It had seemed just as natural when he'd turned into the kiss, and their lips had met.

It had been a mistake. She had a list of reasons why. At the top of the list was Colby. He needed her. She doubted herself. When nothing was making sense or working out, how could this possibly be the right thing?

The library was starting to fill up. Tanner glanced at the paper in front of him, a letter sent by Fletcher, letting them know that the Silver Star had to be in compliance. They had a duty to keep the community safe. He wanted to blow it off, ignore it, but he couldn't. Fletcher knew the law. He knew how to make problems for an organization that wanted to do good.

Tanner shoved the letter aside and leaned back in his chair just as Macy walked through the door with Bea. He'd noticed earlier that Macy looked tired today. But that was the last thing a man ought to say to a woman.

He noticed everything about her. When a man was trying to maintain a professional relationship with a woman, he shouldn't notice her smile, or the way her eyes translated every mood. He also noticed that the tightness in his chest loosened up a little when she smiled a greeting.

He took a deep breath and relaxed.

Gabriel walked through the door, tense as a mountain lion about to pounce. He moved to the end of the table and then paused and turned toward the door as Fletcher entered. The two stared each other down. Fletcher lost that match. His gaze shifted, and he adjusted his tie and quickly took a seat at the opposite end of the long table.

Macy was still standing, looking unsure. Tanner pulled out the chair next to him. She glanced around the room, as if looking for a better option. When she found none, she moved in his direction. Across the table from him, Mayor Elsa Wells peered at him from over the top of her glasses. In her fifties, she'd been his Sunday school teacher twenty years ago. And he guessed she still felt the need to keep him on the straight and narrow. At least that was what he would surmise from the look she was giving him.

A lesser man might have flinched under the fiery look from the redheaded mayor of Haven. He managed a smile.

"Let's bring this meeting to order." Gabriel Everett didn't have his gavel, but his voice was firm, and everyone knew to end their personal conversations.

The door opened, and Seth Jacobs, from a ranch close to Waco, hurried in. Behind him was Lena Orwell from the neighboring community of Fieldton. She served as treasurer of the group. Seth was the LSCL secretary.

"Sorry I'm late," Seth said as he took a chair on the opposite side of the table. "I've been doctoring cows with pinkeye."

Gabriel sat down in his seat at the end of the table. Tanner leaned back in his chair and waited because a quiet Gabriel Everett was a dangerous Gabriel. He let his gaze slide to the other end of the table where Fletcher was looking a mite uncomfortable. He had to guess he was severely outnumbered in this ridiculous task of trying to destroy an organization that had helped so many kids.

"I'd like to start this meeting by discussing Fletcher's claims." Gabriel drilled his gaze into Fletcher, and the lawyer at least had the sense to look chastised.

"These are not claims," Fletcher started. "These are facts. The incidents of violence are on the uptick, and it is only a matter of time before someone gets hurt."

"And you know it is tied to the boys ranch, how?" Gabriel asked.

Fletcher leaned forward, his gestures mirroring Gabriel's.

"I know it is tied to the boys ranch because the crime in Haven is generally low. It is steadily getting worse…"

Tanner couldn't take any more. "Fletcher, crime is getting worse everywhere."

"Fine, if that's what you think. I believe the boys at the ranch are hurting our community."

"Then what should we do about it?" Gabriel jumped back into the conversation. "We aren't closing the ranch, so try to come up with something else."

Fletcher let his gaze drift around the table, from person to person, more than likely looking for anyone who might be on his side.

"I only know that we have to do something. We can't allow our community love of that place to interfere with the safety of our citizens."

Bea cleared her throat, and Tanner knew that look on her face. She was about to blow. He guessed a person could say what they wanted or do what they wanted to Bea, but they'd better have sense to leave the boys on the ranch alone.

"Fletcher, I've just about had it with your nonsense. One time a few years ago a boy soaped your windows. You haven't gotten over that. And maybe it's time you forget and forgive something that was really just a silly kid prank."

"I had to replace—" he started with a sputter, and then he waved his hands. "That has nothing to do with this. I want our community to be safe."

"And I want to change lives. As do the other people in this room. When or if you find evidence that incriminates one of our boys, you let me know."

Gabriel cleared his throat and looked around the room.

"Well, I guess that takes care of that. Now we'll discuss our searches for the missing alumni of the ranch."

Fletcher stood, pushed his chair in and stared them all down. Tanner didn't mind at all. He gave the local attorney the same look, daring him to really say too much.

"I think you all will regret this." With that, Fletcher turned and left.

"Wow," Macy said. "I guess he's not a fan of the ranch."

"That's an understatement," Katie Ellis added.

Gabriel rapped his fist on the table. "We need to discuss our searches. Anything new to share?"

Tanner pointed to Macy and drew Gabriel's attention to her. She raised her hand just slightly.

"Macy? You were searching for Avery Culpepper?" Gabriel jotted down a note on his paper.

"Yes, and she called me." Her words hung in the air, and a murmur spread through the room and then died down.

"And?" Bea pushed.

"She's actually very eager to come to Haven. I explained that she doesn't really have to get here so quickly. But I think she might show up sooner rather than later."

Bea murmured, "Thank You, God."

"How do we know we have the right people?" Lena Orwell asked, a pencil stuck behind her ear and her red hair a bit of a mess.

"We'll have to check identification and backgrounds," Katie piped up.

Lena pulled the pencil out of her hair and tapped the table. "We'll just have to be careful."

"We will be," Bea assured her. "And I have a lead on Samuel Teller. He has actually donated to the ranch. It's been several years, but I don't think he'll be hard to find."

"Anyone else?" Gabriel asked, looking first to ranch foreman Flint Rawlings and then momentarily to Tanner. And Tanner got it. No one wanted their skeletons dug up.

Flint shook his head. "I'm following a few leads, but so far nothing."

Tanner shook his head. "I'm still looking."

Before he could say more, a loud ruckus ensued. Footsteps sounded in the hall, and someone shouted. Gabriel hurried to the door. He opened it to one of his ranch workers.

"Something wrong out there?" Gabriel asked, his normally unflappable demeanor in evidence.

"Yes, sir, someone put a rock through the windshield of Miss Bea's car."

Tanner pushed back his chair and stood. They were miles from town, and very few people, other than the ones in this room, knew about their meeting. This was definitely getting personal.

Gabriel turned back to the room. "I guess this meeting is adjourned. Bea, let's go see what's going on."

They were all standing, moving toward the door, and Tanner realized Macy was next to him. She was planning to walk out the door with the rest of them. And he couldn't let her do it.

"Do you think it might be a good idea if the women waited inside until we see what is going on?" Tanner suggested, knowing the women would protest and maybe even rebel.

Gabriel glanced back, but then he came to a dead stop in the hall. "I do think that's a good idea. Something we all need to remember is that, so far, no one has been hurt. And we don't want that to change. I agree with Tanner. The fewer people we have out there, the better."

"It's my car, Gabriel." Bea moved to stand next to the man. "You can tell the rest of them to stay. Or you could ask, because I know these women, and they don't want to be ordered around."

Gabriel gave the group a long, steady look. "If you all don't mind waiting inside, I'm going to check Bea's car and probably call the police."

"I need to go," Macy said, not really objecting but not really acting as if she intended to agree with the plan.

"We can't keep you safe if you leave," Tanner told her. "Considering the fact that your car was tampered with last week, I think it would be better for you to stay until we know there's no one out there."

All eyes were on them, and he couldn't seem to care what people thought, or even what they would say. He stood face-to-face with a woman whose green eyes were unsure. Her mouth was a firm, stubborn line.

While they lingered there, Gabriel headed outside with a half dozen people following him and Macy still shooting daggers because he'd tried to stop her from going out that door.

"You're not my keeper," she said when they were alone.

"No, I guess I'm not. I just want to keep you safe. Colby needs you."

"I know that." Her resolve weakened. He could see it in her expression. "I don't want to let him down."

"No, of course you don't." He led her to the front door. The group had gathered around Bea's car. Obviously they were going to ignore his warning that they shouldn't all be out in the open.

"Who do you think would do this?"

Tanner led her down the steps and across the lawn. "I don't have a clue. But it seems it has escalated since the details of Cyrus's will were revealed."

"Someone who doesn't want a boys ranch?" She stopped to look at Bea's car with its cracked windshield.

Someone who didn't want a boys ranch. The words, the accusation, were loud and clear. One person didn't want the ranch. One person knew where they were today. Fletcher.

But one thing Tanner knew about Fletcher Snowden Phillips—he supported the law. That didn't mean he wouldn't break the law, but Tanner couldn't see him going to this extreme.

Tanner took Macy by the elbow and led her to the car he and Flint had delivered to her place the previous day after she'd left it at the ranch.

"I don't think Fletcher would do this," he assured her. "That doesn't mean you're wrong. Maybe the right theory but the wrong person."

"Yes, maybe." She looked up at him, green eyes serious as she bit down on her bottom lip. Her blond hair framed her face, lifting a little as the breeze picked up. The herbal scent perfumed the air.

He let out a breath and took a step back from her and from temptation. "I think it's safe to go." Safer if she left than if she stayed, he decided. She smiled, as if she knew.

Chapter Nine

There were no clues about who might have thrown a rock through Bea's windshield. But the incidents were putting a damper on the entire moving process. People in the community were concerned. People at the ranch were more concerned. They all cared about the safety of the residents. They were also worried about public opinion, always such a tenuous thing.

Macy pulled up to Cabin One on Wednesday afternoon. She and Colby were scheduled for family therapy with Eleanor Mack. Macy had a list today. There were some issues to tackle. She felt it was time. After all of these months of struggling and grieving, it seemed to her that in the past few weeks Colby had been improving.

For herself, she struggled between wanting Colby home so they could move on with their lives together and worrying that she wasn't the mom he needed. Those doubts were magnified after the visit she'd had the previous evening with Laurie Waye. The other lady had stopped by Macy's house to have coffee and talk. She wanted to know how Colby was doing, and how Macy was settling in. During the visit she'd revealed that at one time Cynthia had mentioned the Wayes taking custody of Colby. She went on to say they'd obviously made the best decision, though. It was clear Macy loved her nephew and he loved her. As she'd left, Laurie had offered her help, should Macy ever need it.

The cabin dog, a mutt of unknown breeding but with a sweet face and wiry brown hair, met her as she got out of her car. His tail thumped, and he whimpered as he pushed up against her.

"Hey, Paulie, good to see you, too." She brushed a hand over his wiry head, and he looked up with limpid brown eyes. "Yeah, you have a tough life."

The front door of the cabin opened. Colby grinned at her, his sandy-brown hair a mess, his eyes sparkling. With unshed tears?

"Aunt Macy, you're here."

"Of course I am." She wrapped him in a hug and kissed his head, but then she smoothed down his hair. "Did you think I wouldn't be here?"

He shrugged and then ran off, leaving her to follow.

Eleanor greeted her with a smile and an easy hug. "Good to see you, Macy."

"Is he crying?" she asked, watching after her nephew.

Eleanor gave him a minute to get out of earshot. "He was a little upset. He watches the clock, and sometimes he is afraid that you won't show up. Let's go in the playroom."

Of course he was afraid. Macy ached on the inside, thinking of him waiting for his parents to come home that night. And they never made it. Instead she'd shown up in the middle of the night. He'd been asleep on the couch, the babysitter holding him tight.

They had so much to work through.

The playroom served many purposes. The boys did play in the big room with shelves, boxes, a foosball table and television with game sets. It was also the room used for counseling sessions.

Colby was already in the room. He drew on the chalkboard wall. First he drew a dog. Probably Paulie. And then he started drawing his family. Him, his mom, his dad. As an afterthought, a woman with long hair. Macy guessed it was probably her. He wiped a hand across his parents.

"Colby, why did you erase your picture?" Eleanor asked.

"Because they're gone, and they aren't coming back."

Eleanor sat on the edge of a nearby table and motioned Macy to a chair. "No, they aren't. And how does that make you feel? Use your 'I' words, please. I feel…"

"I feel angry. I'm mad at them for leaving. I'm mad, and sometimes I'm sad. And I have nightmares."

"I'm sorry." Eleanor pulled up a small, kid-sized chair and sat. "How do you feel about Aunt Macy?"

He glanced back, and then he shrugged and started drawing again.

"Colby?"

"I feel like she doesn't want to be here."

Macy closed her eyes and shook her head. "Oh, Colby."

"Macy, tell Colby how you feel about that."

"I wouldn't be anywhere else. Colby, I love you."

"Why do you think your aunt Macy doesn't want to be here?" Eleanor asked.

"Because."

"Because why?" Eleanor prodded.

He wouldn't tell her. For the next five minutes very little happened. Eleanor let him draw, and then she pulled him back into the conversation.

"How do you feel about going home?"

He shrugged.

"Can you draw your house, Colby?" Eleanor asked. "Is there anything you would change about your house? Maybe there are things you would like to get rid of. Or things you would like to get. Some people don't like white walls. They might want blue or brown. Some people like red or blue furniture."

He drew a dog in the middle of his house.

"You would get a dog?" Eleanor asked. "What if Aunt Macy wanted to get new furniture or different pictures for the walls?"

He shrugged, but this time he looked back, as if remembering her presence. "What do you want?"

"I don't know, Colby. I just thought it might be fun if we redecorated."

He nodded and turned to draw a picture of a cat. Macy laughed a little. It felt better than crying.

"So the changes you would make would be animals?" Eleanor asked.

"Yep," he said.

"How would you feel about Aunt Macy's changes?" Eleanor asked.

"I guess it would be okay. It's her house."

"No, Colby, it's our house." She wanted to reach for him, but she didn't.

"I live here," he told her. "I live here."

"Yes, you do. But you won't live here forever, Colby. You will go home. Boys always go home.

Once they feel better, they go back to their families." Eleanor touched his arm to get his attention. "You know that, right?"

"Or to new families." He sniffled as he said it. "I didn't want them to go."

"I know you didn't," Eleanor answered. She motioned Macy forward. "But they did. And we can't change that. And it's okay to be sad. It's also okay to be happy. It's okay to have fun. It's okay to love Aunt Macy."

Macy touched his arm. "And it would be okay if I hugged you, right?"

He hugged her, tight. He held on and held on until she thought he would hug the breath out of her. She kissed the top of his head as he let go.

"I think that's enough for today." Eleanor pushed herself up from the miniature chair. "Why don't the two of you go outside? I think we're getting a new horse today."

"Could we?" Colby was already pulling Macy toward the door.

Eleanor laughed. "Oh, I think definitely."

Colby led Macy out to the barn, moving fast for a seven-year-old with short legs. The truck and trailer at the barn looked familiar. Tanner's truck. She hadn't ever realized how much he was around until recently.

As they approached, they saw the new horse, a pretty bay. Tanner led the animal toward the corral. Chloe was with him, and a young man that she guessed might be Russell.

"Let's not rush in too fast, okay?" Macy tried to slow Colby. "The horse is new and may be a little unsure of his surroundings."

Colby gave her a look that said he didn't think too much of her horse knowledge. As they approached the corral, Tanner turned and saw them. He waved, and the horse pranced around him.

Chloe smiled when they stopped next to her, first at Colby and then at Macy. "Hey, Colby, you're the first one to meet Captain."

"Do you think I can ride him?" Colby asked.

"I'm sure you can. Not today, though. He'll have to get settled in."

Colby looked at the horse and then at Macy. "Aunt Macy, do you know how to ride?"

She shook her head. "No, Colby, I don't ride."

"We'll have to fix that," Chloe said. "Tanner, Macy doesn't know how to ride."

Tanner led the horse in their direction. "That's a big problem, Macy. You can't live in Haven and not know how to ride."

The young man with them returned from the barn. He smiled at Macy and winked at Chloe. "I put away the tack."

"Thank you." Chloe beamed. "Macy, have you met my fiancé, Russell?"

"No, I haven't." Macy held out her hand. He took it in his. The handshake was brief and nothing that would recommend him. She didn't want to make a snap judgment, but she didn't like him.

And from the look Tanner gave him, he felt the same way.

She met his gaze, and something passed between them. It felt strangely right and frightening all at the same time. Right because she knew the chemistry, had felt it in his arms. She felt it when she trusted him with her fears. It was frightening because she thought she wasn't passing this test of motherhood. It was frightening because she remembered the night her fiancé, Bill, had thrown everything away because he didn't want to give up his life. That was how he'd put it. His life. His dreams.

All her life she'd felt confident. She hadn't tackled anything without believing she could overcome it. But this parenting thing was a whole different ball game. And she was learning that doubt could snowball and touch every area of her life if she allowed it.

As her gaze collided with Tanner's, the doubts grew and got tangled up with fresh emotions she hadn't expected.

As they stood next to the corral, Tanner had to shift his focus from Macy and Colby to his sister's fiancé. Russell was tall and lanky, with dark hair a little too long. And he didn't impress Tanner, but he was trying to step back and stop judging. Chloe was right; he'd run off a few boyfriends of hers. Usually for good reason. But she was old enough to make some decisions—okay, maybe all decisions—on her own. She was also old enough to make her own mistakes.

"So, about those riding lessons." He turned his attention to Macy, because it was easier, less complicated. No, he took that back. It was possibly more complicated. "You don't ride?"

"Only if you count the carousel at the fair."

"I don't think that counts," he said. And he regretted it. She was all city. From her new boots to her manicured nails, she was as far from country and what he needed to focus on as a woman could be.

And yet...

"I think it's time you try a horse that does more than go in circles," Chloe said, taking her fiancé's hand.

Tanner turned away because he couldn't focus when he was thinking how happy he would be to send Russell on down the road. He was about to respond when one of the newer ranch hands, Jay Maxwell, came out of the barn and into the corral. Jay was good with the horses, better with the kids. He was going to school to be a therapist, but he liked the ranch and wanted to work in a residential setting.

"Want me to take the horse and put him up?" Jay offered as he reached for the lead rope. "I'll stick him in a stall tonight and put him out in the field tomorrow."

"That should work. Thanks, Jay." Tanner patted the horse on the neck and watched as Jay led the animal away.

"Colby and I should go. Eleanor suggested a walk," Macy explained as she started to back away. And that was when Tanner decided he wasn't ready for her to go.

"About those riding lessons," he pushed.

She stopped. That had been his goal.

"I don't know about that."

Colby yanked on her hand. "But I can ride. If you can, then we can go together."

He watched her pause and consider her nephew's words. Her green eyes focused on the little boy, and her smile was gentle, full of love for the little guy. Finally she nodded.

"Okay, riding lessons."

Colby practically danced a jig. And she laughed, although a bit tensely.

"Friday, late afternoon at my place," Tanner told her. "And don't forget to wear boots."

"I won't forget. We should go."

Tanner opened the gate and walked through,

ignoring the curious looks of his sister. "Mind if I walk with you? There are a few trails that are best. And you want to be…"

Safe. He didn't say it. But with the recent incidents, she didn't need to be away from the ranch alone.

"You don't have to," she told him. She reached for Colby's hand. "We'll stay close."

"But I want to show you the spring. There are big fish." Colby was pulling on her hand. She shook her head, and he stopped.

"I can get a pole out of the barn," Tanner offered.

"Fishing?" Her eyes got big, and she looked as nervous as she had when he mentioned learning to ride.

He barked out a laugh. "Let me guess, you haven't been fishing?"

"Not by myself. Not with, what? Worms?" She made a face, half disgust, half fear.

"Yeah, worms," Colby said with a little too much excitement.

She closed her eyes, scrunching them together. When she opened them, she managed a tight smile. "Okay, fishing. But you're going with us, right?"

"I'll bait the hooks," Tanner assured her.

"Well, I guess I'm going to leave now." Russell stepped away from their group.

The abrupt statement took Tanner by surprise and distracted him from Macy and Colby. He looked past Russell to his sister. She looked just as surprised and not too happy.

"I was going to show you around," she said, not letting too much emotion into the statement.

"Yeah, but I remembered that I have somewhere I have to be," Russell, the gem, informed Chloe. "Sorry, honey, gotta run."

He kissed her cheek. She pulled back. "Fine, go. I'll see you later."

"Of course you will."

"I'll go in and get the fishing gear." Tanner glanced at his sister, giving her what he hoped was an encouraging, not judging, look. "Sis, you want to go fishing?"

She was watching Russell as he walked toward the main house and the old truck he'd parked there. She shook her head. "No, I don't think I do. I'm going back to the shop. Should I close up for you this evening?"

He looked at his watch. "I might be late. So, yes, if I'm not back, go ahead and lock up. Tell Larry I'll be there all day tomorrow."

She nodded and started to leave. Jay must have settled the horse and left the barn by the side door. He was heading in their direction with a backpack.

"Hey, Chloe," he called out, stopping Tanner's sister from leaving.

She looked back, and he held up the backpack. "Did you leave this in my car?"

Her eyes widened. She didn't quite look guilty, Tanner thought. But she didn't look innocent. The ranch hand, probably a guy Chloe would have given a second look if not for Russell, appeared completely innocent but a little confused. He headed her way.

"Interesting," Macy whispered. She was standing next to him, her arm brushing his in an easy way that felt a lot like friendship. "Did you see that coming?"

"I'm not even sure what I'm seeing. She looks cornered, and he looks clueless."

She chuckled. "Well, men usually are."

He looked down at the woman next to him, and she lost that amused look. "I promise you, some of us are not clueless."

She opened her mouth, a lot like those fish Colby was wanting to catch. But before she could say anything, Chloe returned with the backpack, and Jay was heading toward the cabins, whistling a country song.

"Did you do that?" Chloe pointed a finger at Tanner.

"Do what?" Okay, now he was clueless.

"Did you put my backpack in his truck? Because if you did…"

"Why would I?"

Chloe let out a sigh and looked a little lost. "I have no idea. But it was in my car."

"Unlocked car?" Tanner asked.

"Yeah, of course. I never lock my car. He went down to his truck to get some special salve he has for one of the horses, and my backpack was in there. Fortunately it has my name on it because it's one I used in college."

"Maybe it dropped out of your car and someone saw it and just put it in the nearest vehicle?" Macy offered what sounded like a reasonable explanation.

"I can't imagine that." Chloe gave the bag a look. "It was in the backseat. And to make things better, he said Russell saw him take it out of his truck."

"What did Russell say?" Tanner asked.

"I guess nothing. He just saw it." She hooked the backpack over her shoulder. "I'm going, but if you find out anything, let me know."

"I will," Tanner assured her.

When she left, he headed for the barn. "I'm going to get the fishing gear."

He wasn't clueless, but he definitely could use some clues concerning everything going on around this ranch. He would guess the backpack didn't end up in Jay's truck by accident. Someone, other than him, must have the idea that Chloe and Russell weren't a good fit.

The thought was amusing until he realized that the same someone thought he and Macy looked like a couple.

Chapter Ten

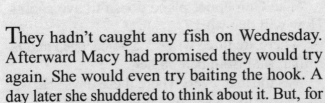

They hadn't caught any fish on Wednesday. Afterward Macy had promised they would try again. She would even try baiting the hook. A day later she shuddered to think about it. But, for Colby, she would try. She just hoped today wasn't the day. She had worked at the local library in the morning and the school in the afternoon. Now she was heading to the ranch to help pack.

Some people thought of small towns as slow-paced and lazy. She'd never been so busy.

She pulled up to Cabin One. Eleanor was sweeping the front porch. One of the boys was picking up a few bits of paper and trash that had blown into the yard. Macy joined them.

"Are you here for the joy of packing?" Eleanor asked, leaning the broom against the wall.

"Whatever you need me to do," Macy offered.

"We need to start packing up toys and summer clothes. I have tubs that we can put them in and a permanent marker for labeling. The boys are going through things, deciding what they can do without for the next few weeks. You'd be surprised how much they're willing to give up. And I'm willing to give up all the dishes. We usually eat a few meals here, as a family, but we'll be eating all of our meals at the main house for the next couple of weeks. Until the move."

"The Culpepper place doesn't have cabins. How will that work?"

"There are three wings," a voice, deep and familiar, said from behind her.

Was the man everywhere these days? He was like a sore toe. She didn't used to notice him, but now she couldn't help bumping into him every time she turned around.

She had to face him, or she'd be a coward.

"Good afternoon, Tanner." There, she'd sounded nearly normal.

"Afternoon, Macy, Eleanor. I volunteered with Russell—" he grimaced as he said it "—to take a load to the Culpepper place. Do you have anything to load up here?"

"We do. I have the laundry room piled with boxes of nonessential items."

"I'll back the stock trailer up there and start loading." He tipped his hat, as if that were the end.

Colby came running out of the cabin, letting

the screen door bang shut behind him and earning him a warning look from Eleanor. But he wasn't running to Macy. She realized that as he hurried past her to tug on Tanner's hand.

Tanner smiled down at him. "Hey, Colby."

"I dug up more worms."

Tanner chuckled at that. "Did you? Well, now, we'll have to see if we can put those worms to good use. But first we have to work. We're going to move some things over to the new ranch."

The smile on Colby's face dissolved into a frown. "I don't want to move."

Tanner looked from the boy to Macy and then to Eleanor. "Why wouldn't you want to move?"

Colby shot Macy a look and then leaned closer to Tanner. "Because I want to stay here."

"But you can't stay here forever. It's a good resting place, Colby. But you have a home."

Eleanor left the porch and moved forward to do what Macy should have known how to do. But she didn't. She was so consumed in Colby's pain, in his loss, that she didn't know what to do for him.

"Colby, there are changes in life. Some of those changes are harder than others. Some changes are good and even fun or exciting." Eleanor knelt down in front of him. "There's something I want you to do for me."

"What?" He didn't manage to sound happy.

Eleanor ruffled a hand through his hair. "First, try to sound like my friend Colby. You are a tough kid. And that's good because you've gone through some tough things in the last year. But I want you to think about going home."

He shook his head emphatically.

"No, now listen. When you think about going home, think about the fun stuff you and Macy will do. Think about that dog you want. Or a cat. Think about what you'll name it. Think about how you want to redecorate. Or what sports you want to play. Think about the future and everything awesome you want to do. You might want to visit your grandma in Arizona. I heard that the Grand Canyon is amazing."

"Maybe we could visit her in the summer. After school." Macy moved toward her nephew, praying he wouldn't reject her.

He didn't. He looked up when she spoke, and he nodded. "I want to go to the Grand Canyon. And ride a donkey."

She held her arms out, and he gave her a hug. "But to do that, Colby, we have to work on being a family."

His little face fell. "I know."

A hand touched her back, comforting. The touch was strong and sure. "I'll touch base with you later?"

"Yes, of course."

Tanner looked around for his helper, who hadn't shown up. "I guess Russell isn't going to make it."

"Maybe we could ride along with you. Colby would probably like to see the Culpepper ranch. And the two of us are pretty good at moving boxes."

"Sounds like a plan. I'll get my truck and back the trailer up to the back door."

They were loading boxes when Jay showed up.

"Hey, Tanner, I've finished with the boys and their new calves. Do you all need help with these boxes?"

"Since our help skated out on us, that would be good. How did your interview go with the school?"

"I think I'll get the job. High school history and geography. And once I finish my counseling degree, I'll be able to volunteer at the ranch as a therapist."

Macy handed Tanner a box and made eye contact with him. It was easy to see what he was thinking as he looked at Jay Maxwell. He was seeing a young man with potential and comparing him to Russell. She had to agree, Russell would probably break Chloe's heart. But she also knew from experience that Chloe would have to learn that on her own.

Her phone rang as they were loading the last box. She stepped away and answered it.

"Hey, Macy, it's Avery Culpepper. I wanted to let you know, I've gotten things taken care of here. I'll be in Haven by Sunday."

"Like I said before, I'm not sure that it's necessary to come right away, but you will be able to meet with the lawyer and have a look around town."

"Oh, I plan on staying."

"Well, if you do, we have several options," Macy offered, realizing she wasn't going to be able to talk Avery out of coming to town now. "There's a boardinghouse, a B and B, and just down the road in Fieldton, there's a hotel."

A long pause and then a quiet "Oh."

"Do those not work for you?"

"Well, I kind of thought, since I'm Cyrus Culpepper's granddaughter, that I would stay at his ranch."

"That might be a problem, and I definitely am not the one to give permission for that."

"I am his heir."

"Again," Macy said as Tanner turned his attention to her and the phone call, "I'm not the one to give permission for that. There is a will. And lawyers."

"I see. Well, wasn't my granddad a rich old coot?"

Macy opened her mouth, and she just couldn't get the words out.

"Hello?" Avery sounded young and immature.

"Yes, well, I don't know anything about your grandfather and his finances."

"I guess I'll be getting myself a lawyer, then."

"That's probably a good idea." Macy made eye contact with Tanner. "If you're coming to town Sunday, we'll be at church. If you want to meet me there at noon, I can help you find the boardinghouse or the bed-and-breakfast."

"I'm certainly not going to church," Avery countered. "But, yeah, okay."

"Okay." Macy ended the call. "Wow."

"Avery Culpepper?" Tanner asked.

"Yes, and she's going to be a mess. She wanted to stay at the ranch."

"That is a problem." He motioned her toward his truck. Jay was already inside with Colby. "Climb in. I think we're ready to take the first load."

"Okay." She got in. "I don't know what I expected from Avery."

He started the truck and eased forward. "I guess we expected her to be decent. Old Cyrus was as ornery as they came, but he was a good man. Decent."

"When did his son leave?" Macy asked.

"I'm not sure if I ever knew his son. So I guess long before I ever came to town. Lila at the café said the two of them had a falling-out.

She doesn't know if they ever spoke again, but she said Cyrus always regretted the way they parted. He even hired a private investigator to find his son. I guess the PI must have learned about the granddaughter, but he didn't find her before Cyrus passed."

"What a shame."

"Stop!" Colby shouted from the backseat. "Stop talking about Cyrus."

Macy shifted in her seat to look at her nephew. "Colby, what's wrong?"

"I don't want to talk about Cyrus and his son. And I don't want you to talk about him dying."

"No, of course not. And we won't talk about it anymore."

Jay had a hand on Colby's arm, and the two started talking quietly. Macy faced forward again, giving them as much privacy as she could in the cab of a truck. A hand covered hers. She moved, letting Tanner's fingers wrap around hers. It had been a long, lonely year.

Tanner parked with the trailer backed up to the front porch of the Culpepper house. He'd been here a few times, but he was always impressed by the size of the place. Chloe could call his house a castle, but by these standards he lived in a cottage.

"This place is huge," Colby said as he hopped out. "Like a mansion, right?"

"Kind of," Tanner agreed as he looked up at the place. It needed some work, but there was a fund for that. They would need more beds, more food, more of everything.

"Can I go inside?" Colby asked as he stepped up onto the porch.

"You sure can. But stay close to us." Tanner opened the back of the stock trailer. "And grab a box."

Colby grumbled, but he grabbed a box. Jay went next. They carried the boxes inside and up the steps to the floor designated for Cabin One and the Macks. The old place was still in good shape. There were hardwood floors but some carpet. The bathrooms were plentiful, and that was important with an operation of this size.

"Let's use this front bedroom for storage," Tanner suggested. "I think it will end up being a living room of sorts."

They put the boxes against the wall and then headed back down to the trailer for the next load. As they walked out the front door, Tanner noticed a truck coming up the long driveway. When it got a little closer, he realized it was Flint Rawlings from the Silver Star.

"Flint, did you come to help unload boxes?" he asked the foreman of the boys ranch.

Flint stepped onto the porch. And he wasn't smiling. "No, afraid not. I just got a call from the Lawrence Ranch foreman."

The Lawrence place shared a property line with the Silver Star. Tanner knew the place well. At one time he'd tried to buy it.

"Yeah?"

"They've had a horse stolen. One of their therapy horses."

"Great." Tanner walked away from Macy and Jay. Flint followed. "And I suppose they want to blame the boys?"

"Yeah, they do. In all of the years I've worked at the ranch and lived in Haven, I've never seen anything like this. A community that used to support the ranch now seems bent for leather in shutting it down."

"We'll do some serious PR work in the next couple of months. Katie Ellis is good with fundraisers and public relations." Tanner rubbed a hand down his cheek. Great, he'd forgotten to shave today. He whistled. "This is all getting a little dicey."

"Yeah, and there's more."

"Of course there is."

Flint pulled him farther away from the others. "Russell was out there the other day. And he had them show him this horse. He said he was thinking about buying it for Chloe. Of course, they told him it wasn't for sale."

"Russell couldn't buy a stick horse for Chloe."

"That's what I figured. I'm not saying he stole the horse. I don't know if he has the brains for being a horse thief." Flint grinned as he said it. "But if not, someone else did. And with everything else going on, I think we have to do more to figure out who is sabotaging the school."

"Local law is getting nothing?" Tanner asked as they headed back down the porch.

"Nope. There just isn't any evidence."

"So what do we do?" Tanner watched as Jay, Macy and Colby grabbed more boxes from the trailer and headed back inside.

"I have a friend who might be able to help. I'll get in touch and get back to you. I'm just not sure if he's willing. He has some history around here and with the ranch."

"I'm not sure if we need anyone else with a vendetta coming into the picture, Flint," Tanner said as he walked into the trailer.

"He won't have a vendetta. I just don't know if he'll want to help. And who has a vendetta?"

"It would seem that whoever is causing these problems does."

Flint shrugged. "The one person I know who has an imaginary beef with the ranch is Fletcher.

And I can't believe he'd have the nerve to pick up a gun or a rock."

Fletcher. The name hung between them, and they both shook their heads and said, "Nah."

"By the way, Macy found Avery," Tanner informed the other man as they carried boxes up the steps.

"That's great. One down and four to go. I hope you're having more success than I am."

Tanner shook his head. "Nope. Gabe's grandfather is nowhere to be found. I have one lead, and I don't think Gabe is going to like it."

"Why do you think Cyrus did this? Why couldn't he just give the place to the kids and let it be? Instead he had to attach all of these conditions. Finding people. Having a big celebration. There are kids at stake here."

Tanner set his box down on top of the others that were being stacked against the wall. "I'm not sure. Cyrus could be ornery, but he wasn't a bad old guy. Maybe he wanted people to see how well the boys of the ranch turned out. Fletcher seems to want to stir the other pot, and make the boys all look like juveniles."

"Yeah, maybe that was it. I know that Samuel Teller has sent quite a chunk of cash to the ranch. And Cyrus supported the ranch, too."

Macy reappeared with another box. "Everything okay?"

Flint shrugged and left Tanner to decide if he should tell her or not.

"A horse was stolen from a neighboring property," he said. "And of course it makes the boys look bad. But also, Russell was there the other day, asking about buying the horse for Chloe."

"You think because he wanted to buy it, he might have stolen it?"

"I don't know what to think anymore." He motioned her ahead of him, and they started down the stairs together.

The house was monstrous with big rooms and floor-to-ceiling windows. There was a main wing and then two wings ran back from each end of that main building. The ceilings were high. The woodwork was custom.

"It's going to be expensive to heat and cool," he mused as they walked out the front door.

Something streaked past them, a flash of black-and-white. Macy shrieked and jumped to the side. She let out a pained groan and hopped back to lean against the wall.

"What happened?" Tanner was at her side, a hand on her arm. "Are you okay?"

Stupid question. Of course she wasn't. Her eyes were closed and her mouth tight with pain. Before she could answer, Colby ran at her, his arms going around her waist.

"I'm okay, Colby. I think I stepped on a nail. What was that, a skunk?"

"A cat," Tanner supplied as he took her by the arm and led her to the porch swing. "Let's take a look."

She reached to pull off her shoe. Or what a woman considered a shoe and he considered a scrap of canvas. Blood was already seeping out. From behind him, Jay held out a towel.

"Me and Colby are going to take more boxes upstairs." Jay had Colby in hand. Tanner was glad of that.

"It's fine, Tanner," Macy murmured as she dropped the shoe. "I really liked those shoes."

"I think calling those shoes is using the term *shoe* pretty loosely."

"Be quiet." She grimaced as he lifted her foot. "It's pretty deep. When was your last tetanus shot?"

"Does it count if I don't remember?"

He wrapped the towel around her foot. "I think if you can't remember, it means you need one."

"I can do that tomorrow."

"I don't think tomorrow will work." He stood and held out a hand. "Come on. Let's take Colby and Jay back to the Silver Star, and I'll drive you to Fieldton to the urgent care."

"You don't have to."

"Oh, you're going to drive yourself?"

"Well, I..." She shook her head. "No, I guess not. I just don't want to be a bother. I'm sure you have other things to do."

"You're not a bother. Let me help you into the truck." He put an arm around her waist, and she leaned into him, her arm around him.

They took a few hopping steps forward, and he realized it wasn't going to work.

"What?" She looked up at him and tried to take another step.

"This," he said. He turned her, and then he scooped her up in his arms, ignoring her protests. He carried her to his truck. "Open the door."

"I could have walked," she grumbled as she reached for the handle.

"And then what kind of knight would I have been? Colby would have been disappointed."

She leaned into his shoulder as he placed her on the truck seat. He tried to think back to the last time he'd held a woman and been tempted to not let go. But with her arm around his neck and her cheek against his shoulder, it was worth thinking about.

Chapter Eleven

"I don't have time to be on crutches," Macy complained as Tanner helped her through her front door that evening.

He didn't say anything, but he flipped on lights and moved her in the direction of the sofa.

"It's a nail hole," she continued. "Who would have thought jumping out of the way of a skunk…"

"Cat," he corrected.

"A cat, then, would have resulted in this."

"Jay said he found the nail and hammered it back through the porch."

"Good. I wouldn't want one of the kids to step on it." She propped her foot up on the coffee table.

Tanner grabbed a throw pillow, lifted her foot and slid the pillow under it. "There, that will be more comfortable. And you're on crutches because the puncture was deep."

"But only for a few days."

He sat on the nearby recliner. "What do you want for dinner?"

"I'll heat up a bowl of soup."

He stood. "I'll heat it up."

"You really don't have to do that." She grabbed the crutches, and he pointed a finger at her.

"Stay."

"Of course." She would stay until he wasn't looking.

He headed for her kitchen. She could hear him banging around in the cabinets. And then the radio came on, and country music drifted through to the living room. She finally did get the crutches under her arms and head for the kitchen. He didn't say anything, just tossed a look back as he emptied the contents of two cans into the pan on the stove.

"Water or tea?" he asked when he finished. "And I told you to stay."

"In school I always got marked down for not following instructions." She patted the chair next to hers. "I really appreciate you helping me today. I could have done this alone, but I'm glad I didn't have to."

"So am I." He sat next to her. Their shoulders brushed, and she could smell the spicy, outdoor scent of his cologne.

It was one of those colognes that made a woman

want to lean in close to a man. It might even have been one that would make her want to touch his face, experience his kiss.

As if he knew what she was thinking, he leaned in, cupping the back of her head. And then his lips were on hers, and she was experiencing something she'd convinced herself to be a fluke. But it wasn't. This was real. What she felt when he held her was the most genuine thing she'd ever experienced with a man. It felt pure and good, and it felt dangerous.

He moved back, whistling as he let her go. "I should leave now. Is there anything you need?"

She smiled at the question and reached to touch his cheek, to run her fingers through the thick hair at the back of his neck. And then she pulled back, reminding herself that this wasn't the right time in her life for relationships.

"No, I'm good. And thank you."

He dished out a bowl of soup, placed it in front of her and gave her a spoon.

"I could call Chloe to stay the night with you. Or Josie Markham?"

She shook her head. "I'm really okay. I have some things to do around here. Maybe now I'll stay in one place long enough to do those things."

"I understand. Call if you need anything."

"I will. Thank you."

He left, and she was alone and feeling more

lonely than ever before. Funny how that had happened, and all because he'd kissed her and shown her some kindness.

She finished her soup, managed to get the bowl in the sink, and then she headed for the office next to the bedroom she'd claimed when she moved in. She'd avoided Grant and Cynthia's bedroom. It felt like a shrine. In all the time she'd lived there, she hadn't been able to touch anything of theirs. There were shoes by the closet door, discarded by Cynthia; maybe she'd decided the silver sandals didn't match her outfit. Or maybe they'd been uncomfortable. Cynthia's perfume was still on the bathroom vanity.

Macy bypassed the office and headed for the bedroom. Maybe it was time to start letting go. If she let go, maybe she could move forward.

She pushed the door open and entered the room. It still felt wrong, as if she was entering a domain in which she didn't belong. The few times she'd been in here, she'd felt as if her brother and sister-in-law would come home and catch her in the act of going through their belongings. Each time that thought had sent her back out of the room.

And so it had remained, much as it had the night she first arrived in Haven. The night she'd gotten the call from the hospital.

She pulled a chair close to the dresser and sat

down. One drawer at a time. She pulled out the top drawer and sighed. Jewelry, notes, mementos. She'd rather go through clothing.

A knock on the front door saved her from going through a box of papers. She grabbed the crutches and hobbled to the living room. It was eight o'clock in the evening, and with everything happening in the community, she didn't open the door the way she might have done a few months earlier. Instead she tiptoed forward and peeked out.

Chloe waved from the front porch.

Macy opened the door to the younger woman and motioned her inside. "You really didn't have to come. I told Tanner I'll be fine."

Chloe looked a little bit surprised. "Tanner?"

"He didn't send you?"

Chloe shook her head. "No. Was he supposed to?"

"Let's get a cup of coffee. And, no, he wasn't supposed to. He took me to the doctor this afternoon, and he thought I should have someone here with me."

"Someone other than him?" Chloe guessed.

"I really don't need anyone," Macy insisted. "It was sweet of him."

"He can be sweet," Chloe said with a tightness around her mouth that took Macy by surprise.

"Tanner didn't send you." She sat down at the kitchen table. "So something is wrong."

"No, not really. Or maybe." Chloe sat down across from her. "My brother is overprotective. He has a difficult time letting go."

"Yes, I told him he should give you space."

Chloe cocked her head to the side. "Did you?"

Heat crawled into Macy's cheeks. "I guess that isn't my place."

Chloe grinned. "Well, it isn't. But it's interesting that Tanner is taking advice. Anyway, I left the house. He was upset about the horse missing from the Lawrence ranch. And of course Russell is being blamed."

"Was he with you today?" Macy asked, pushing herself to her feet. "I'm still hungry. Do you want to share a pizza with me? I'll put one in the oven."

"I'd love to. And, no, he wasn't with me. I'm not sure where he was."

Macy glanced back as she hit the power button on the oven. Chloe looked unsure, but Macy wasn't going to point that out. If the other woman had doubts about her fiancé, she'd work it out.

"You can stay here tonight," Macy offered as she pulled the pizza out of the freezer.

"I'd like that. It looks as if we could both use a friend."

Macy thought that was an understatement.

Chloe had an older brother trying to guide her but with maybe too firm a hand. Macy had a room full of memories to sort through.

They both had decisions about their futures that needed to be made.

Friday afternoon, Tanner pulled away from his ranch, the Rocking B, and turned his truck in the direction of the farm supply store. He'd spent the morning separating steers that were heading to the livestock auction. The next thing on his list was to check a shipment that had arrived at the store. Larry had called to tell him there was a pretty good ding on a new tractor.

Chloe was just pulling in as he got there. She'd called last night from Macy's place to let him know she wouldn't be coming home. He'd tried to apologize. She'd told him it wasn't necessary. She understood he was worried about her future. But he needed to let her make her own decisions and trust that she'd make the right ones.

They parked next to one another and met up in front of the building. "Hi, big brother." She looked up at him, shielding sunshine from her face with her hand.

"Chloe. Everything okay at Macy's?"

"She's good. She decided her foot feels better, and she isn't using crutches. I told her she'll be sorry."

She would. But like his sister, she wasn't going to listen to him. Not only that, she wasn't his to order around. Macy would make her own decisions, and either it would work out or she'd suffer for it.

He didn't want her to suffer.

"That's a fierce look," Chloe teased.

He opened the door and motioned her inside.

"I have a lot on my mind. Lane called to tell me he'd heard the price of cattle is going to drop. And then Larry called to let me know a tractor that was special ordered has a dent."

"That isn't good."

"No, it isn't." He followed her behind the counter. "If you have this, I need to make a few phone calls. I'm afraid I've found a lead on Gabe's grandfather."

"Not good news?"

"No, I don't think it is. And later I'm supposed to go help search for this missing horse."

"Russell didn't take it."

He looked up from the packing list. "Okay."

"I know you think he had something to do with it. He was in Waco. Remember, he has a job."

"I'm sure if they need to check his alibi, they will."

"Okay. But remember to give a person a chance before you start accusing."

"I'm trying, Chloe. I know you don't believe that, but I want to like the guy. For your sake."

"Thank you."

"This is just a tense situation. We have the move for the boys ranch and now someone intent on causing problems in the community. I'll be glad when things are back to normal."

Chloe came around to stand behind the counter. "I was at the café this morning. You know, there are people accusing Fletcher. Because he's so against the boys ranch."

"I know. I'm finding it hard to believe he would go as far as this, to shoot at buildings and put children in danger."

"Yeah, I told them I didn't think he was the person responsible."

"Hopefully we'll catch them before we have the whole town up in arms." He pulled his phone out of his pocket. "Flint just texted me. He heard they found where the fence was cut on the Lawrence ranch."

Chloe didn't look up at him, and he wasn't about to question her. If she doubted her fiancé, that wouldn't be something she wanted to talk about.

When she didn't respond, he filled in the silence. "I'm going to make this call, check that tractor and then head out to the Silver Star. We've got less than two weeks to get these kids moved."

"Let me know if there's anything I can do." Chloe looked up, her expression guarded. "And, Tanner, if Russell did this…"

"One day at a time, sis."

"Yes, of course."

Tanner left his store a short time later. On his way to the Silver Star, he stopped by his place. His foreman, Lane, had called to tell him the buyer for the gray horse, Frosty, was due anytime.

Lane came out of the barn, wiping his brow with a handkerchief. "Hey, boss, didn't expect you back so soon."

"I was driving past and decided to stop and make sure Frosty is ready to meet his new owners."

"I just brushed him out, and he's in a stall waiting. I hope they like that rotten thing."

"He's showy. They'll like him." Tanner closed his truck door. "Just be honest about his temperament. Why don't you bring him out now and work him a little so he calms down? I want them to see him at his best, but also explain that he's dramatic."

"Sure thing."

Lane brought the gelding out of the stable on a lead rope. The animal was a little on the excitable side. It shied at every noise, even at a gust of wind. Tanner didn't think Frosty was that nervous, but rather that he liked the drama of shying and kicking up his heels.

"He's a crazy colt," Lane said. "If he's alone, he never even startles."

"I'm sure he'll settle as he gets older."

"True that. These people have an older daughter. She's an experienced rider, and this horse won't bother her a bit."

"I saw her showing Western pleasure last year. She can handle Frosty, or I wouldn't consider selling him to her. Hey, did you tell me about a neighbor with puppies to give away?"

"You looking to get a dog, boss?"

He ignored the question.

"Yeah," Lane answered when he didn't get a response from Tanner. "The Jacksons have a litter of mutts. I think the mama is a collie, and the dad is a retriever."

"Weaned?"

"Yeah, about ten weeks old. Cute little things. I got one for my niece."

"Thanks. I think I'll go and leave you with this. If you have any problem with the buyer, let me know."

"Will do. Hey, have they found the Lawrences' gelding?"

"Nope." He headed for his truck, checked the

time and drove off in the opposite direction he'd planned to go.

When he pulled up to the Jacksons', Melton was outside. The old farmer wore his customary bib overalls, one strap hanging loose. He had on rubber boots up to his knees and a fishing hat.

"Tanner, what brings you to this side of town?"

"I heard you had puppies to give away."

"Yes, I sure do. I've got three left. Do you want them all?"

"No, I think I'll just take one."

With a grin, Melton headed toward the barn, and Tanner followed. The puppies were inside with their mom, a pretty black, tan and white collie. Two of the puppies were fawn-colored; one looked like the mama dog. He picked that one up, and it licked his hand.

"Melton, I think I'll take this puppy off your hands."

"Chloe will like that one, Tanner."

Chloe. He felt a little guilty. "No, this one is for one of the boys at the ranch. For Grant Swanson's son."

Melton Jackson's smile faded. "That little boy ought to have a puppy. That was a bad situation."

"Yes, it was."

"I guess his aunt is going to stay?"

"I'm assuming she will."

Melton hitched up the strap of his overalls that

hung loose. "I guess I wasn't sure if she'd stay in our little town. It would be a shame to take that little guy away from his home and everyone he knows."

Tanner nodded at the statement, but he couldn't brush off the way it cut deep, the idea of Macy leaving. He was used to people leaving. But Macy? He guessed he wanted her to be a person who stayed.

For Colby's sake, of course.

The puppies that were left crawled around his legs, sniffing and whimpering. He reached down and picked up one of the pale pups that looked a little like a golden retriever.

"Melton, I think you're right. I think Chloe needs a puppy."

By the time he got to the Silver Star, he was calling himself every kind of fool. Those puppies were all over the cab of his truck, and from the smell in the backseat, one of them had had an accident.

He wasn't surprised to see Macy's car parked out in front of the main house. She was probably packing up the library or finishing up grants.

As much as he'd thought a puppy was a good idea, now he wondered if he'd lost his mind. He reached in the backseat and grabbed up the two menaces before heading inside.

The front foyer and parlor were deserted. Built near the same time as the Culpepper place, the Silver Star had some of the same architecture, though on a smaller scale. High ceilings, crown molding and tall, narrow windows.

"Anyone here?" he asked as he headed through the house. Near the kitchen he heard Bea, and then she stepped out of what had been a storage closet.

"What brings you to the Silver Star, Tanner?" She saw the puppies, and her eyes widened. "I hope you haven't brought me a gift. The last thing I need is to potty train a puppy."

"No, I wouldn't do that to you, Bea."

"Who would you do it to, then?" she asked.

He held up the fawn-coated puppy. "This one is for Chloe."

"For accusing her fiancé of horse thieving?" Bea asked.

"Thanks for not beating around the bush," he told her as he held up the other puppy. "This one is for Colby Swanson."

"I'm sure Macy will thank you for that. She's out at the barn. I guess Flint is teaching her to ride while she waits for visiting hours with Colby."

Flint was teaching her.

Something that felt a lot like jealousy shot

through him. He pushed it aside. It didn't matter who taught her as long as she learned.

And after last night, he ought to be glad he wasn't involved.

Chapter Twelve

Macy knew her legs were shaking as she sat atop the big, rusty-red gelding named Bud. Flint had assured her that no other horse could be trusted the way he trusted Bud. The twenty-year-old horse had taught a lot of kids to ride, he'd informed her, including his own son, Logan, who was six.

When they first started, she'd thought Bud shook harder than she did. The horse had calmed down. Macy had even managed to take a few deep breaths. Flint shook his head as she rode the horse around the arena.

"If you want, we could call the local fair and get you a carousel horse," Flint offered from his place leaning against the corral fence. She was glad he was the only witness. "I can ride this horse. Colby is going to be proud of me."

"Of course he will be," a familiar voice said, not Flint's.

She turned, and the horse turned with her. And kept turning. She grabbed the reins, and the horse started moving backward.

"Stop jerking the reins," Tanner called out in a voice too calm, she thought, for the situation. A quick glance and she saw that he was grinning.

Stop jerking the reins. Easy for him to say, but she didn't know how to stop. Flint had told her, to stop the horse she had to pull back. She was pulling back. Flint moved forward as Bud started to circle again.

"Macy. Stop. Don't pull back. Don't move. At all." Tanner's voice had a healthier dose of concern.

She let the reins go. Bud stopped. Flint was moving back away from the horse, but he didn't do a very good job of hiding his amusement. And then Tanner was there, taking hold of the reins.

"Pulling back like that is a command for him to back up," Tanner explained. "And when you jerk the reins around, you're turning him."

"I didn't jerk," she protested. "Did I?"

He moved his hand over hers. "A light rein against his neck, and he's going to move. Steady back and he'll stop. And use your knees. You'll get it."

The bundle of black, white and tan in his arms whimpered.

"You have a puppy." On closer inspection, she noticed he had two. "Two puppies."

"Chloe is coming out here later. I wanted to surprise her."

She leaned closer, running a hand over the soft coat of the puppies. "Ah, how sweet, bribing her to forgive you for being an overbearing older brother. I had one. He didn't approve of my relationships, either. And in the end, he was right. Amazingly enough, it worked itself out."

"I know that she'll make the right decision."

"Bravo, you can say it, even if you don't believe it." She unhooked her foot from the stirrup and moved her toes inside the boots that were a size too big. "I'm going to admit something, and you'll enjoy knowing that I was wrong."

"What's that?" he asked, handing the puppies off to Flint.

"I'm sure I can't get off this horse, and I know that when I do my foot is going to hurt."

"I happen to own a castle and have my own kingdom, so rescuing is second nature."

"Corny, but useful." She eased her right leg over the saddle and held out her arms. Tanner reached for her, put his hands on her waist and lifted her off the horse.

"So who is the other puppy for?"

He took the tri-colored puppy back from Flint and handed it to her. The ball of fur wiggled in her hands, and when she lifted it close to her face, it gave her chin a bath.

"It's adorable."

"It's for Colby," he told her, sounding very confident about that fact.

"No!" But she was still holding the puppy, and it was now licking her hand. "We can't have a puppy. I don't know anything about dogs. Or cats. Or—" she looked at the horse that had moved to nuzzle her arm "—horses. I know nothing about horses."

"There's only one way to learn, Macy. Sink or swim."

"Puppies are a big commitment. They take a lot of time." She held on to the wiggling mass of fur with its cold, damp nose and tongue that seemed intent on licking her entire hand and arm. "Even I know they take a lot of time."

"Yes, they do. But it seems that this one likes you."

Yes, the puppy liked her. And she was sure she liked it. She knew Colby would love it.

"What do I do with it?" She cuddled it close. "Does it stay inside or out? What about food? And do I house-train it?"

"It can be inside or out. It eats Puppy Chow. And, yes, it can be house-trained."

She rubbed a cheek against the puppy's head and fought the wave of pain that rolled over her heart. "Tanner, I'm not even sure if I can raise a little boy."

"You are raising him, Macy. You're making the hard choices even when it hurts. I think that's parenting."

"I'm not so sure."

"Trust me."

She did. And now it was time to change direction before her heart got tugged any closer.

"And you're going to help me with this puppy?" She looked up at him, the puppy wiggling to get down and the horse pushing against her arm, begging for attention.

"I'll help you."

"Thank you. Then I guess I should go introduce Colby to his new puppy."

Flint took the reins of the horse. "I'll put this guy out to pasture."

"Thanks, Flint." She gave Bud a final pat on the neck because it hadn't been his fault she didn't know what she was doing.

"For what it's worth, there's nothing like a dog for a young boy," Flint said. "My son, Logan, and his dog, Cowboy, are best friends."

She smiled and said, "Thanks. I think." And then she shifted her attention back to Tanner. "What are you doing out here?"

"I'm out here to help look for the gelding that wandered off from the Lawrence ranch."

"And here I thought small towns were quiet and maybe a little boring."

"Not lately, it seems." He took her arm and

guided her from the arena. "What was it that doctor at the urgent care told you?"

"It seems I can't remember. I'm fine, really. A little sore, but nothing I can't handle.

They exited through the gate, and he turned to latch it. And then they stood there for a moment. In the distance kids played. The puppy squirmed and whimpered in her arms. A soft breeze blew, rustling the drying leaves in the trees. He did love Texas Hill Country.

"Your sister thinks you're trying to end her relationship with Russell." She put the puppy down and watched as it wandered a short distance from them. "Jay called and asked her if she would help him with a horse he's trying to break. Because someone told him she's the best."

"And of course she thought it was me." He whistled, and the puppy trotted back in their direction.

"There, he's already trained."

"I think that was more curiosity than obedience." Tanner reached to pick up the puppy. "I didn't tell Jay anything about her ability to train a horse."

"I didn't think you did." She took the puppy from him. "We should introduce Colby to his new friend, unless you have to leave."

"I've got a few minutes."

She pulled out her phone and looked at the

time. "Visiting hours start in five minutes. We can head toward Cabin One."

"Do I need to carry you?" he asked, one corner of his mouth tugging up.

"I think I can make it."

She did take the arm he offered, leaning a little on him as she clasped her fingers around his muscled forearm. She liked this rancher, she admitted to herself as they headed across the big lawn in the direction of the cabin.

If only it was a different time and a different place.

Tanner stayed back as Macy climbed the steps of the cabin and knocked on the door. This was her place, not his. Colby was her nephew, and Tanner was the bystander. He needed to take more than a physical step back. He needed to take an emotional step back from her, and from Colby.

The last couple of weeks had proved that it would be too easy to become involved. And she'd admitted it herself, she didn't fit here in Haven, on the ranch. She didn't know if she could be the person Colby needed.

He couldn't imagine a relationship with a woman who couldn't be a part of his life. He'd seen too many of those marriages, with the man going one direction and the wife going another.

Separate interests, separate lives and with kids somewhere in the middle. It rarely worked.

Eleanor answered the knock on the door. Her mouth dropped when she saw what Macy held in her hands. A minute later Colby appeared. The little boy let out a whoop and took the puppy. Macy glanced back at Tanner, including him.

Good intentions fell to the wayside. Her look pulled him forward, drew him in, made him a part of their moment.

As an honest man, he could admit, he liked being in their lives. Colby held the puppy up for him to see.

"Tanner brought the puppy, Colby." Macy reached for Tanner's arm and pulled him close. "Can you tell him thank you? For the puppy and for helping us housebreak it."

"Good one. Very good." He shook his head as she quickly put him in the middle of the situation. "Do you like him, Colby?"

"Yeah, I do. I'm going to name him Sir Arthur. We were reading a story about him in school."

"That's a great name. Can we call him Arthur, for short?" Macy asked.

Colby kissed the puppy's head. "Yeah, I think so. And when I come home, he can sleep with me."

At the mention of home, Tanner noticed tears

shimmering in Macy's eyes. She blinked them away and nodded. "Yes, you can sleep with him."

Colby looked up. "I think that's good. I'm used to Sam being in my room."

"I know you are."

Colby hugged the wriggling puppy. "Sam's dad is really mad that he's here. Sam said his dad said mean things."

"I'm sorry, Colby." Macy got down on her knees, putting her close to her nephew. "Life is tough sometimes."

"Yeah, but we're tough and getting tougher." He grinned as he said it.

"You are so right. I didn't realize I was this tough. Did you?" she asked.

Colby shook his head, and then he leaned into her shoulder.

"I want to come home," he whispered close to her ear.

Tanner's throat tightened, and suspicious moisture covered his own eyes. He blinked and looked away. He hadn't cried in a long, long time. He should have known it would take a seven-year-old boy to reduce him to tears.

"I think I'll leave the two of you to get acquainted with your new family member," he said, reaching to help Macy to her feet. "I'll drop supplies off at your house. And I'll see you both at church Sunday, if not sooner."

"Do you have to go?" Colby asked.

"Afraid so, Colby. I have to get work done."

"I'm putting a roast in the Crock-Pot. For lunch after church on Sunday," Macy said, and it sounded like an offer.

"If that's an invitation, I accept."

"It's an invitation." Her hand rested on his arm.

"Then I'll definitely see the two of you Sunday."

Her hand dropped from his arm. "Tell Chloe she's invited, too. And don't forget, Flint has her puppy."

"I'll get him before I head out."

This was all starting to feel a little sticky. As he got in his truck a few minutes later, Chloe's puppy struggling to be free from his arms, his thoughts returned to Macy and Colby. They were filling spaces in his life that he hadn't realized were empty.

He left the Silver Star and headed for the Everett Ranch. Gabriel was in the equipment barn working on a tractor. Tanner leaned in to see what his friend was doing.

"Anything I can do to help?" he asked, holding tight to the puppy that he had on a makeshift leash Jay had made for him.

"Yeah, you can tell me to stop being sentimental over a piece of metal and buy a new tractor."

"I can help you with that. I have another shipment coming in next week."

Gabriel crawled out from under the tractor. He wiped his hands on a grease rag. "So, what brings you out here today? Seems to me you've been spending a lot of time at the Silver Star."

"Is there a question in that?"

"No, not really. More of an observation. Good thing you have about the best ranch foreman in the state." Gabriel's slight grin set off a warning bell. "And you have a puppy."

"Okay, an observation. What's your point?"

"You and Macy Swanson. Never thought I'd see that. I kind of thought you were looking for a woman who could drive a tractor and pull a stock trailer. Isn't that what you told me?"

"I'm not looking for a woman. Period. And I'm definitely not letting you fix me up again."

Gabriel laughed at that. "I have to apologize. Clarice was not at all what I expected when I introduced you."

"Me, either. I thought I wouldn't get out of that alive."

"She kind of stalked you for a while after, didn't she?" Gabriel looked far too amused.

"A little. Thanks for the reminder. The nightmares had almost stopped."

Gabriel shook his head at that. "Well, I like Macy."

"So, date her." Tanner said it, but he didn't mean it.

"No, I don't poach. And I'm not interested." He led Tanner to an old cola cooler from some bygone-era gas station. "Want a bottle of water?"

"Sure."

Gabriel lifted the lid of the cooler and took out two bottles.

"I know you're not here to sell me a tractor." Gabriel sat down on a bench next to the cooler.

Tanner sat next to him, holding tight to the puppy that plopped down to chew on the rope tied around her neck. "About your grandfather. I'm assuming you want updates."

Gabriel took a long drink of water before answering. "Yes, I do."

"I haven't found him. I'm sorry about that."

"Me, too. But I didn't figure you would. If he'd wanted to be found, he would have shown up a long time ago."

"Maybe so. What I have found is that he had a record. He did a few stints in prison, for petty stuff mostly. Short incarcerations. I haven't found anything recent. The last mention of him is about fifteen years ago when he was released after a year in state."

"We have to find him, Tanner. Not for me. I stopped expecting him to come back about twenty years ago. But the ranch needs for us to find him. I can't let the boys at the Silver Star down."

Tanner got that. The boys ranch had saved

Gabriel Everett the same way it had saved Tanner's brother, Travis. Gabriel had worked long and hard to keep the ranch afloat.

"More beds means more boys having the opportunity at a new life." Gabriel said what Tanner already knew. But he didn't interrupt. "You're not giving up."

It wasn't a question, but Tanner felt an answer was needed. "No, I'm not giving up. We'll find him. And I guess you've heard that Avery Culpepper called Macy."

"I heard. Macy called Bea. And it seems Macy is a little troubled by Avery's behavior."

"A little. I think Avery is under the impression she's an heiress."

"I'm sure once she gets here and we explain, she'll understand."

"I hope so."

Tanner got up to leave. "I have to run to the store and get puppy supplies for two puppies." He grimaced as the words slipped out.

Too much. Gabriel arched an eyebrow and waited.

"Colby wanted a puppy. It's about starting over and…"

Gabriel held up a hand. "You don't have to explain."

No, he didn't have to explain. He picked up Chloe's puppy and walked away. It wasn't his most manly exit ever, with the puppy wiggling and licking his face.

He ignored Gabriel's parting comment, telling him he was getting in deep. He didn't need to be told.

Chapter Thirteen

The two vans belonging to the Silver Star were pulling into the church parking lot as Macy got out of her car on Sunday morning. She waited for them to park and then for Colby to get out. He spotted her, said something to Eleanor and headed her way.

"How's my puppy?" he asked as Macy hugged him.

"He's good. He said to tell you that he loves your bed."

Colby laughed at that. "He didn't sleep in my bed."

"No, he slept in his own doggy bed that Tanner bought him."

"Tanner bought him a dog bed?" Colby took her hand, and they started up the sidewalk to the church.

"He did. A dog bed, food, a collar and a leash.

We'll have to take Arthur to Doc Harrow for his shots."

"He has to get shots?" Colby paled a little. "Why?"

"Well, because just like boys, dogs can get sick. We want to protect him from diseases."

"Can I go?"

"We'll see." She turned as a car pulled into the parking lot of the church, the engine of the red convertible loud and rattling.

The woman behind the wheel of the car was a blonde. From the tint, probably not natural. Definitely not natural. As people turned to watch, she got out of her car and combed fingers through dry, brittle hair that had almost a hint of green to the pale shade.

"Uh-oh." Chloe came up behind Macy. "Is that our Avery Culpepper?"

Bea appeared next to them. "Don't tell me."

"Avery Culpepper," Macy and Chloe said simultaneously.

"If that's Avery, she's early." Macy watched the woman dig around in her car. "And she said she wouldn't be here for church."

"She has green hair," Colby whispered.

All three women put fingers to their lips and told him, "Shh."

Avery stood next to her red convertible, her hair now covered by a Western hat with a big feather hatband. Her jeans were tight. Her boots were bright pink. Her shirt was pink satin with fringe.

"Oh, my." Bea chuckled. "That girl found a Western store on her way to town and they had relics from the *Urban Cowboy* days."

"John Travolta called, and he wants his..." Chloe started and then giggled. "Seriously, that's bad. Even Macy didn't try that hard to fit in."

"Gee, thanks." Macy looked down at her own boots. "My boots look just like yours. As a matter of fact, I bought them at your farm supply store."

"My brother's farm supply store." Chloe rolled her eyes dramatically. "Here she comes."

Avery, or they guessed she was Avery, headed their way, arms swinging and mouth chomping on gum. She saw them waiting and grinned big, waving as she climbed the steps.

"Hey, y'all, I'm Avery Culpepper. I got a call from someone saying I'd inherited a ranch."

The ground fell out from under Macy. "I didn't say that."

Bea put a hand on her arm and stepped forward, taking control. "Avery, my name is Beatrice Brewster and I'm so sorry for your loss."

"Loss?" Avery stopped smacking her gum and managed to look a little bit sad. "Yes, when I heard about my grandfather, I knew I had to head on over here. I wish I could have known him."

Her blue eyes, rimmed with dark blue and silver eye shadow, watered in a convincing-ish manner.

"Yes, of course. He was a dear man." Bea patted Avery on the back. "Tomorrow morning you can talk to his lawyer. Harold Haverman has an office here in town. You'll find he can help you with everything."

"And do you have a key to the ranch so I can have a place to stay?" Her gaze landed on Macy. "Are you the one who called me?"

"Yes, I'm Macy Swanson. As I told you on the phone, you'll have to find a place here in town. The bed-and-breakfast might have a room." Macy added a smile to help ease things along.

"I seriously have to rent a room? I thought that was a joke." Avery's sweet sentimental act disappeared. "I was under the impression I had a ranch."

Bea's smile slipped away. "No, my dear, your grandfather had a ranch."

"Which is now mine because I'm his only living relative." Avery turned her attention back to Macy. "You tell this lady I'm his heir."

"Avery, I told you that your grandfather had passed away and you are in his will. If you'll remember, I didn't mention the contents of the will or the stipulations. This will all take time, and we'll have to verify that you are indeed the granddaughter of Cyrus Culpepper."

"If I can't stay at my ranch, where will I stay?"

Macy started to say something about it not being her ranch, but Bea put a hand on her arm. "I'll give you the number for our local B and B."

The church bell was ringing, and Colby was pulling on Macy's hand.

"Church is about to start," Chloe chimed in, her tone far too amused.

They entered the church, and Macy relaxed a little. The interior of this building, with its warm tones, wood pews and the smell of citrus, always did that for her. Chloe led her to a pew near the front. Only as she sat did she realize she was sliding in next to Tanner.

Their arms brushed. He scooted to make a little more room. Colby climbed on her lap. It felt right to have him in her arms. It felt right to be in this church. No matter how complicated things had been, maybe she did have a life here in Haven. Maybe she would become a part of this community.

For the past year it hadn't always felt that way. The majority of the time she'd been more tempted to go than to stay.

Her gaze shifted forward to where the Wayes were seated with their family. The family Grant and Cynthia might have planned for Colby to be a part of if something should happen to them. And yet, here she was. She hugged Colby close, holding him tighter than a boy of seven wanted to be held. But she needed a minute with him in her arms.

The music started; the hymns took the roof off that old building when everyone sang. But even with raised voices, she could hear Avery Culpepper asking someone if her grandfather had actually attended this church. Next to Macy, Chloe chuckled. Tanner shot her a look.

The music ended, and the sermon started. Macy tried to focus, but Colby had fallen asleep, and he was heavy. Somewhere behind them, Avery still commented from time to time. And all around them people were wide-eyed and shocked.

Cyrus had been ornery, a little bit of a hermit, but his granddaughter was something else.

With the final amen, they all stood. Avery was at the back of the church, standing with Fletcher Snowden Phillips. He was nodding as she spoke. And then he took her by the arm and led her out of the church as he pulled his phone from his pocket.

"That can't be good," Tanner said.

"No, I don't think it is. She's still determined to call herself an heiress."

"She's not going to be happy," Chloe offered.

"No, she isn't," Tanner said as he took the groggy Colby from Macy's arms. "He's got a pass today?"

Macy nodded. "Yes. He can't wait to get home and play with Arthur."

"We're still invited for lunch, right?" Chloe asked.

"Of course. I even made a pie." She glanced around the parking lot for Avery. "Since I found her, should I do something to help her? It feels strange that I was her contact person and I'm not doing more."

Tanner nodded toward Fletcher's car, where Avery stood. "I think Avery has found a friend. It isn't a good friendship, but at least she's being handled."

"I think that's the last person you want her talking to," Chloe offered. "I don't understand that man."

"None of us understand him." Tanner opened the back door of Macy's car for Colby to get in. "We'll just hope his good side overcomes, and he stops fighting the moving of the ranch."

She hoped Fletcher had a good side. But she didn't comment. As they stood there talking, she noticed curious glances directed at them.

People whispered and nodded. They were being seen as a couple, she and Tanner.

But they weren't. Couldn't they just be friends?

* * *

Macy's house smelled like roast and baking bread. Tanner followed Chloe inside. He noticed that Macy had taken down a few pictures, replaced throw pillows and added flowers.

"What do you think?" she asked in a quiet, hesitant voice.

"It looks a little more like you." By that he meant warm and welcoming. But he didn't want to say it.

Colby stood next to him, a little wired up. "Want to see Arthur?"

"Of course I do. Where is he?"

"Aunt Macy left him in the backyard. He likes it out there. And Aunt Macy said you brought him a doghouse. That makes him almost like our dog and yours. We can share him."

"I think he should be all yours," Tanner said. But he let Colby lead him through the living room to the dining room and the French doors that led to the deck and the fenced backyard. Arthur was waiting for them.

They played with the dog while Macy and Chloe made the decision that it was too nice a day to eat inside. He watched as they set the table and then brought out the food. Macy had pushed the button on the side of the house, and the porch awning slid out to cover the table area, giving them shade.

On any given Sunday it was just Chloe and Tanner for lunch at the ranch. Sometimes they went to the Candle Light. Every now and then they drove to Waco for lunch and shopping. Lately Chloe had been missing, choosing Sundays to go out with Russell.

"Time to eat," Macy called out. She was filling glasses with iced tea.

Tanner motioned Colby to follow him. "Let's wash our hands."

"Ah, man." Colby looked at his hands. "They aren't dirty."

"No, but you've been playing with the dog."

"He cleaned my hands," Colby said with a mischievous grin.

"Yeah, he did." Tanner put a hand on Colby's head. "You've got me there. But if we don't wash our hands, Macy will pull our ears."

"She wouldn't pull our ears." The boy led Tanner inside. They were alone in the kitchen, hands in the sink, when Colby spoke again. "My aunt Macy is really nice. And I hope you are nice to her. Because that guy Bill yelled at her."

Tanner pulled his hands back and reached for the towel.

"Bill?"

"She was going to marry him, but then he yelled a lot and left."

Tanner knew he shouldn't ask. He definitely

knew better than to get involved. He usually knew better, he corrected.

"What did he yell about?"

Colby grabbed the towel to dry his hands. "Me. He didn't sign on to be saddled with someone else's kid."

And then the little boy hurried out of the house, leaving Tanner with more questions than answers.

Lunch was easy. They talked about the Silver Star, about the arrival of Avery Culpepper, and Arthur. Tanner fought the urge to ask Macy about Bill, a man who had made a little boy feel small and unimportant.

And, no, Colby hadn't said it. But the reality had been there in his eyes and his hurt tone. Tanner had to wonder if losing his parents and then overhearing what Bill had said might have been what pushed Colby Swanson to the level of anger that had seen him placed at the ranch.

He would talk to Macy, later. When they could be alone.

He looked up and caught her watching him. Alone. He guessed that was a bad idea. Her lips were pink and kissable, and he couldn't stop imagining the way it felt to hold her.

Maybe he would just mention the conversation with Colby to Eleanor and let her handle it.

No, he wouldn't do that. Macy deserved to

know. Even if it put him in the bad position of having to tell her.

"Everything okay?" she asked as they cleared the table.

"No," he responded. She stopped moving, holding the empty meat platter in her arms and waiting.

"What's wrong?"

"We need to talk. About Colby."

"I have to take him back to the ranch soon. I bought posters for him to put on his walls. We're going to do that first. But if something is wrong, you need to tell me."

"It's about the past. Nothing you can fix right now."

She moved away from him, cradling the platter, her shoulders stiff. He followed her inside. He hadn't handled this the right way. Maybe because he didn't want to get involved. He wanted to give her the information and let her do what she needed to with it.

"Chloe, could you take Colby out back to play with his dog?" Tanner asked as they entered the kitchen.

Chloe was washing dishes, and she gave him a look that said he'd lost it. Colby got up off the floor where he'd been sitting with the dog.

"Sure, why not?" Chloe turned off the water and

looked at Colby. The little boy grinned, grabbed his dog and followed her out of the kitchen.

"You didn't have to do that," Macy told him as she sat the platter by the sink and rinsed her hands.

"I think I did. I don't want you to be worried all day."

"It scares me that I rely on you so much."

It scared him that she'd just admitted that.

"I guess I never met Bill," he started.

"We ended things soon after I moved here. He hadn't signed on for this, he said. It was supposed to be us starting our lives. We had a five-year and a ten-year plan. A nephew and a move to Haven didn't fit."

"Macy, Colby overheard that conversation."

She shook her head, biting down on her lip. "No. I thought he was in bed."

"I'm sorry."

"Colby didn't say anything. If he had, I could have explained that sometimes things end. They aren't meant to be. And my relationship with Bill was one of those things."

"Tell Colby. He needs to hear that from you."

"I will. I'll talk to Bea and we'll find a time to sit down with him and talk this out. He is the world to me."

Tanner made a move toward her. She stepped

into his arms, allowing him to close her in an embrace. Her head rested against his shoulder.

"You've been strong, Macy. Colby is blessed to have you."

She nodded. "I hope so. I hope I'm doing the right thing, and I hope he can come home and learn to be happy with me."

"I think he's already happy with you. He's hurt and angry that his parents left."

"Yes, and someday he'll understand that they didn't want to go."

"I think he already knows that," he assured her. "Sometimes our mind plays tricks on us, convinces us of things that aren't so."

The words settled between them, and she pulled back as if they had been meant for her.

If she'd intended to say something, she didn't. The back door opened, and Colby and Chloe returned, laughing and discussing the puppy. Chloe was telling him about her puppy and about a pony she'd recently bought just because it was cute. She told him maybe Macy could bring him out to see Lucy, the pony.

Tanner pulled at his collar as he watched Chloe, Macy and Colby discussing ponies and puppies. It was definitely time for him to make his excuses and go.

"Chloe, are you heading out with me?"

She looked at him like he'd lost his mind or had three eyes. "Yeah, I guess. Are we going?"

"I got a call from Flint this morning, asking me to come by the ranch and talk to him. He's at the Culpepper place."

"I guess we can go, then, if you're in a hurry."

"I am, kind of. Lunch was amazing, Macy. Thank you." Tanner noticed the flush of pink in her cheeks. He guessed he noticed a lot about her, after having not really paid much attention for the past year.

"Anytime. We enjoyed having company." Her hand went to Colby's shoulder. The little boy was saying something about Chloe's pony.

They left, Chloe shaking her head as she walked to his truck. He'd driven the flatbed farm truck today. She yanked the door open because sometimes it would stick. Slamming it wasn't necessary, though.

"What?" he asked as he backed out of the drive.

"You are so weird. This is why you don't want me to date Russell, because you don't know the first thing about relationships."

"I do." And he did. He'd come pretty close to proposing to a girl he dated in college. And the two of them had realized they wanted completely different things out of life. He talked to Marcia from time to time. She lived in San Diego and worked in fashion.

"Why the rush to leave?"

"We had lunch. It was good. They had things to do. So do I."

"You're afraid." She narrowed her eyes at him, the way she'd done since she was about three.

"Yeah, I'm afraid." He tried to make it sound like a joke.

His phone rang and Chloe laughed. "Saved by the ringtone."

"Not a saying."

"It is."

"Nope." He answered his phone. "Flint?"

"We've got a problem at the Culpepper place. Someone spray-painted the living room walls. I tried to call Gabe but couldn't get hold of him. You're next on the call list."

"I'll be there in five minutes."

He tossed his phone on the seat.

"What happened?"

"Someone spray-painted the walls of the Culpepper place."

Flint was waiting for them on the front steps of the house. The police were just leaving. Tanner greeted the other man and walked inside, following him to the front living room.

"Nice timing, that Avery 'I want the ranch' Culpepper showed up, and today we have these nice murals on the walls," Chloe said as she walked around the living room.

"I hadn't even considered her," Flint admitted. "Yeah, it is a little coincidental."

"Maybe too much of a coincidence?" Tanner offered. "But we've got to get to the bottom of this before someone gets hurt. What are the deputies saying? Any leads?"

Flint shook his head. "Nothing. They see coincidences the same as we do. But whoever this is, they're not leaving any evidence behind."

"Then we've got nothing." Tanner touched the walls. Completely dry.

"I have that friend." Flint walked up next to him and followed his example, touching the paint.

"Who is this friend?"

"Heath Grayson. We were in the army together. These days he's a Texas Ranger. I know he has some history around here, but he might help us out."

"What can he do that local deputies can't?"

Tanner watched his sister walk out of the room, her cell phone to her ear.

"He's just really good at digging and finding things. Better than anyone I know."

"Talk to him. We'll pay him for his time."

"I don't think he'll take money, but I'll talk to him."

That taken care of, they headed back outside. "Anything you need help with out here?"

Flint pulled keys out of his pocket. "No, I'm done. I was checking fence before we bring livestock next week."

They parted. Chloe seemed upset as she got in the truck.

"You okay?"

She gave a quick, jerky nod of her head. "I'm good."

"Anyone I can hurt for you?"

She laughed, the sound watery. "No, I can do my own hurting. Anyone I can help you see as the woman you should marry?"

"You know, Travis needs to come home so you can spend time torturing him." Tanner patted his sister's hand. "I'd do anything for you."

"I know you would." She finally faced him. She wasn't crying, but she was close.

Yeah, he wanted to hurt someone. He wanted to hurt Russell. He wanted to add a guy named Bill to that list. Because Macy hadn't deserved to be hurt, and the fact that the guy had hurt Colby in the process was inexcusable.

Chapter Fourteen

On Tuesday Macy got to the Silver Star early. The boys, including Colby, were in school. She'd planned it that way to give herself a chance to go through paperwork, pack and do whatever else she could to help. Bea peeked into her office just a little after nine.

"How's it going in here?"

"Good. I think there is a lot of this that can be shredded. I don't see moving paperwork that is outdated and won't be necessary for records. Do you want me to box it so you can go through it first?"

"No, I trust you." Bea pulled up a chair. "Macy, I think it is very close to time for Colby to go home. I think we will move him in about ten days. I'm hoping by next week to have the boys at the Culpepper place, or the Triple C, as they like to call it. I guess that's the real name.

Since Colby is already packed up, I'm going to let you start taking his things home. He can have a pass to help you put it all away. After that we'll do a weekend pass and see how that goes. I do want him to have a gradual transition."

Macy looked down at the papers in her hand, unsure. Really unsure.

"Macy?"

She nodded. "I'm good. I'm just afraid. For him. For me. What if it's me? He's doing so well here with Eleanor and Edward, and I worry that I'll take him home, and we'll find out it's just that I can't do this."

"You've been doing it. You've been the mom, coming here, doing therapy with him, loving him through this. And now that's he's talking about the conversation with Bill that he overheard, maybe we can resolve all of this stuff he's buried and kept to himself. A little guy shouldn't have to carry these burdens."

"A mom should have known how to protect him." Deep breath. She closed her eyes. A hand rested on her shoulder. "We'll be fine. Of course we will."

"Of course you will, or I wouldn't be sending him home with you. I only wish all of our kids were as blessed as that little boy, Macy. So many of our kids will never go home. We hope and pray that they can, but many will stay here until we can find a home for them. I'd worry more if you weren't a little bit afraid."

Macy sighed. "So fear is a good thing?"

Bea nodded. "A little fear can be good."

Chloe stepped into the office. "Hey, did you need me for anything? I got a note from Russell asking me to meet him in Waco for pizza. Opal's Pizza. I've never heard of it."

"I don't think we need you to do anything," Macy answered. "Bea?"

Bea shook her head and got up from her chair, groaning as she did. "Not that I can think of. I need to keep moving, or I won't be able to move. I hate packing."

"Me, too. I'm going through Grant and Cynthia's room this week."

"I wish you'd done that sooner, for yourself," Bea said, stopping at the door. Chloe moved aside to make room for her.

"Yes, I should have. I guess I didn't want to change their home. Colby's home."

"You don't have to change it. Just make it yours. And let go of their belongings. Let Colby help decide what to keep. Maybe you could make a box for him, of the special things he wants. Help him to learn that memories are good."

"Thank you, Bea."

"You're welcome, honey. And, Chloe, you have a good time tonight. Macy, get something to eat. And if you go to town, bring me back some chicken salad."

"I will. I just need to work a little on the grant before I leave."

"Not a problem. Honey, we just appreciate you so much. Your grants have really helped. And soon I won't have to turn away so many boys. I just can't wait to see that ranch overflowing with boys. I just hope that Avery doesn't do something to delay or to take this away from us."

"I do, too, Bea."

Macy left a few minutes later. She stopped at Lila's first, parking on Main Street. As she got out of her car, she glanced in the direction of the Fletcher Snowden Phillips Law Office. The door opened, and a blonde in a sundress and wearing too-high heels walked out, swaying and wobbling as she turned to say goodbye to the lawyer.

Avery Culpepper looked far too pleased with herself. Macy cringed, thinking of the trouble the young woman could cause. Although Cyrus's will had insisted they find her, Macy wished she hadn't.

Lila's wasn't very busy. Macy glanced at the clock. It was early for lunch. And too late for breakfast. She was headed for the counter when she noticed him sitting with his back to her. Dark hair, broad shoulders, cowboy hat hanging on the chair next to him.

"Have an early lunch with me, Macy?" Tanner pushed out the seat across from his with his booted foot.

"How can I turn down an invitation like that?"

"I would hope that you couldn't. It was charming." He handed her a menu.

"Oh, very charming. Here, darling, let me pull you out a seat," she mocked, grinning at the rancher, who had the grace to blush.

That blush nearly undid her. It was sweet.

"How's Colby?" he asked. And not because it was the right thing to do, but because he cared. She knew that.

"He's good. He's going to come home shortly after the move to the Culpepper place."

"That's good news."

"Yes, it is. It really is." She glanced at the menu. He leaned a little forward, making her strangely aware of him, of his scent, of the gentleness in his blue eyes. "It is good. You can do this. And he's going to be just fine."

"I hope. I really do." She took a deep breath. "I do worry that he will be okay, but he would be better with someone else. Someone who isn't me."

"You can't believe that."

"I'm not sure what I believe anymore."

"You know I like you." He said it in a gruff voice, taking her completely by surprise.

She put the menu down. "I like you, too."

"Macy, I'm not a man who randomly spends time with a woman. I want to spend more time with you."

Her heart skittered all over the place as she looked into the dark blue eyes of the man sitting across from her. She wanted to spend forever with him. She nearly choked on the thought.

"I'd like to spend more time with you, too."

"But…"

She'd seen that coming. Bill wanted to marry her, but he didn't want to be a dad to Colby. He didn't want to live in Haven. Tanner wanted a wife, kids and someone comfortable on a ranch in Haven.

"Uh-hmm?" Her heart was pounding in her throat. This felt strangely like a relationship in the beginning stages. Or maybe one about to end before it started. She found she didn't want to lose him.

"But I do feel like we're in different places." Yes, that was what she expected.

"Meaning?"

"I'm settled here. I know that, eventually, I'll get married and have kids."

She wanted to be mad at him for being so right and saying it out loud. "And I'm not settled. I still don't know if I belong here. Sometimes I won-

der if Colby would be better starting fresh somewhere new. Even in Arizona near my mom."

"I know. And I don't want to miss you if you
decide this isn't the right place for you."

"I don't want to miss you, either." She already
missed him, and they hadn't said goodbye.

His hands found hers midtable, and he twined
his fingers through hers. His hands were sun-
tanned, strong and calloused from farmwork.
Dark hair sprinkled on tanned forearms. She
looked at their fingers laced together and saw it
as a reflection of their lives. They'd started on
this journey separate and from different backgrounds and places. Today, sitting there with
him, she could see them as a couple.

"I'd like to see where this could take us. And
I'm not a man who uses those words lightly."

"I know you're not. Give me two weeks. Let
me get Colby home and get our life sorted out,
and we'll take another look."

"I think that's a good plan. But sometime this
week I would like to take you out to dinner."

"If you ask, I'll say yes."

The waitress approached, and he released
Macy's hands. Her heart was another matter.

If Tanner told anyone that he'd practically
asked Macy Swanson to go steady, like some

green sixteen-year-old boy, they wouldn't believe it. He still didn't believe it.

Even as he drove out to the Silver Star to help move livestock that evening, he was still feeling kind of numb. It had been hours ago, yet he remembered the way she'd looked at him with those green eyes studying him, waiting for something more than what he was prepared to give.

What he should have told her was that he hadn't met a woman in years, maybe ever, who made him think about the future the way she did. Being with her, near her, changed everything for him. He no longer saw himself as the owner of the Haven Tractor and Supply, or the owner of the Rocking B; he saw himself as someone who could have a life with Macy, with Colby.

It was amazing that three weeks could change him this drastically. Amazing. And it scared him silly. Because he knew that she might leave.

When he pulled his stock trailer up to the barn at the Silver Star, Flint was coming out, carrying saddles.

"Grab a load," the other man called to him. "I have boys in there helping pack stuff."

He headed inside, and there was Colby, trying hard to drag a full-size saddle down the dusty aisle of the barn.

"Hey, partner, want a hand with that?"

Tongue out, face tight with focus, Colby shook his head and groaned. "I got it."

"I can see that you do. Let me get the door for you."

"Okay," he said, followed by another grunt as he tugged the saddle, trying to haul it up on his shoulder the way he'd probably seen the older guys do.

"Are you ready for the big move?" Tanner asked, grabbing another saddle and following the little boy out the door.

Colby shot him a look over his shoulder that made Tanner think maybe the kid wasn't ready. "I guess."

"Oh, you just guess? Did you know, I saw your aunt today, and she bought a basketball hoop?"

"Yeah, I don't want to play basketball."

"Why not?" Tanner was lost. He'd seen the kid playing with the other boys.

"Because I don't want to go. I don't want to leave Eleanor and Edward and the kids. And I know you like her, and you'll just say mean things and threaten to leave."

"Whoa, hold up there." Tanner set the saddle he was carrying on the tailgate of his truck and took the oversize saddle that Colby was dragging. "Let's talk about this."

Colby fought him, but Tanner picked the boy

up and carried him a short distance away. "I want down."

"You sure do, and I'm going to let you down in…" Tanner paused, taking a few more steps. "In five seconds."

He put Colby down but held him to keep him from running.

"I thought you were excited about going home."

"I changed my mind. I want to stay here. This is my home."

"No, you have a home in town. With your aunt Macy. And she loves you."

"Yeah, she loves me, and that's why Bill left."

He didn't think of himself as slow to get things, but this time it took a few minutes. When he did get it, everything made sense. "Right, okay, she picked you."

"Yeah. I don't like when grown-ups fight."

"Neither do I." Tanner glanced up as Edward approached. He gave the other man a look, asking for help. This was way outside his realm of expertise. He could teach a kid to ride, even to rope, maybe to ride herd on some cattle. Sometimes he could give decent advice. But Colby had a load on his young shoulders that needed more.

"Hey, Colby, what's up with you? I haven't seen you that mad in a long time." Edward sat down on the ground and pulled Colby next to him. Tanner started to leave, but Edward stopped him with a raised hand.

"I don't want to go home. I don't like it when grown-ups get mad, and then they go away and they don't…" Colby crawled into Edward's lap and cried.

"They don't what?" Edward prodded.

"They don't come back. And it's all my fault."

Tanner ran a hand over his eyes and walked away. Colby's pain pretty near ripped a hole in his grown heart, so he couldn't imagine how the little boy felt. Probably how he'd been feeling for a year, since his parents' deaths.

Near the house he saw Macy talking to Chloe. He headed their way because Macy needed to talk to Edward and Eleanor. She needed to hear this from them, not from him. Whatever "this" was.

"Macy, I think Edward is going to need you. He's over by the barn with Colby."

"What's wrong? Is Colby hurt?"

"Not physically."

Macy hugged Chloe and told her to call later, after her dinner at Opal's.

Tanner waited until Macy walked away. "Are you going to dinner in Waco?"

"Yes, I got a note from Russell to be there at seven." She hesitated and he waited. "I guess from Russell. He mentioned this place to me a week or so back, and the note was signed by him. But the handwriting looked weird."

"I'm not sure if that's a good idea." He backed off, hands up. "I'm sorry, that was none of my business."

"No, it isn't." She pursed her lips and stared him down. "Okay, it is your business because you worry about me. But I have to make my own decisions about the person I date."

"It is your choice. Just be safe."

"I will. Is Colby all right?"

"He will be."

Tanner watched his sister get in her car and leave, and then he returned to the barn. He saw Macy sitting with Colby, saw her fighting tears as Colby cried and clung to her. It was hard to stand back and not charge in. He wanted to hold them both, her and Colby.

Every thought like that one took him by surprise. At thirty-two, he hadn't planned on being knocked off his feet by a woman. And yet, here he was, contemplating this city girl, her nephew and how to keep them both in his life.

Eleanor had joined Edward, Macy and Colby. She reached for the little boy, and he went to her, holding tight to her neck. And leaving Macy looking alone and lost. Tanner brushed a hand through his hair and headed the other way.

"We loaded your trailer with equipment from

the barn. Do you want to drive it over to the Triple C?" Jay Maxwell asked as Tanner put distance between himself and Macy.

"Yeah, why not?"

"You okay?" Jay asked, following him.

"I'm good. Tell Flint I'll meet you all over there."

"Will do," he said, but Jay was still giving him a curious look.

"Tanner?" Macy, small voice and waterlogged eyes, stood behind him.

He didn't know what else to do, so he opened his arms. She poured herself against him, heaving sobs racking her slim frame. For a long time he rubbed her back and told her it would be okay. He didn't know how, but it would be okay.

"I don't know what to do for him. He's just broken and so hurt, and I don't know what happened. I wish Grant and I had talked more. If we had, maybe I would have known what was going on. I would have known if they were having problems in their marriage, or if they had a bad night, and Colby felt guilty. I would know how to fix this. I should know how."

"Now that he's started opening up, it's only a matter of time before it all comes out, Macy. And we can pray. For him. For you to know how to help. And for the staff here."

"Yes, I know. I get so caught up in the pain, and I just want to dig our way out of this."

"Understandable."

She leaned into him and sighed. "Thank you."

"You're welcome." He led her toward his truck. "Want to ride along with me?"

"I would like that. I think I can't be here much longer. Eleanor is going to help Colby calm down and put him to bed."

"Let's go. After we get done, I'll take you to dinner."

They were pulling up the drive of the Triple C when Macy's phone rang. Tanner glanced her way as he negotiated the driveway and then the narrow lane that led to the barn.

"Chloe? What's wrong?" She bit down on her lip and avoided looking at Tanner.

Chloe was practically shouting. "He was with another woman. Macy, they were holding hands." Tanner didn't think he heard every word, but he got the gist of it.

"But he invited you?"

"The note wasn't from him. I think I knew that, but I wanted…" The rest was garbled. Tanner clenched the steering wheel and waited for someone to tell him what was going on.

"Oh, honey, I'm so sorry. What can I do?" Macy held the phone tight as if she knew he was tempted to take it. He parked and waited for someone to include him.

He could hear his sister talking. He heard the word *note*. And *over*. Macy looked everywhere but at him.

"I'm here. If you want to stay the night at my place tonight, you can." She cleared her throat. "You should call Tanner and tell him."

He grumbled about that being a sweet idea.

"No, he'll say he loves you." Macy smiled at him. "And then he'll threaten to go beat Russell within an inch of his life."

Another pause, and then Macy spoke again.

"Yes, he is." And she handed him the phone.

He took it, his hand brushing Macy's in the process. He'd been in control for years. A carefully ordered and structured life, the antithesis of what his parents had provided them. And in a matter of weeks, two females and a boy had turned his life topsy-turvy.

He was okay with that. That was the part that really stunned him.

Chapter Fifteen

A cool wind blew, reminding everyone that it was fall, even though they'd had summerlike temperatures for the past week. It was close to the end of October. In less than a week the boys would be sleeping at the Triple C.

Macy had volunteered to help paint one of the new wings, and Chloe had joined her. Josie Markham was there also, but they wouldn't allow her to help paint. She brought water from time to time and then left again. The surprise helper was Jay Maxwell. When he arrived, bringing a sandwich for himself and Chloe, Macy made a point not to ask questions.

"How is Colby doing?" Chloe asked as she dipped the roller in paint and swiped it down the wall.

"He's better. He's still not really talking. I just know he blames himself for his parents' deaths.

He was doing so well, and we were planning what it would be like when we got home, and now he won't talk about it."

Jay set his paintbrush down on the shelf of the ladder and descended to grab a bottle of water. "This happens, Macy. He does want to come home, but there is a fear of not being able to handle it. He probably can't vocalize that at his age, but it happens to older children. The great 'what if' factor. They've been doing so well, but what if when they get home they can't continue their recovery? What if they revert to old behaviors?"

"Eleanor is working with him, trying to get him to confront those fears. We're hoping his trip home this weekend will help."

"And don't be too hard on yourself if there are rough spots." Jay climbed back up the ladder and continued painting.

Macy happened to glance at Chloe and saw the other woman watching him. Interesting. They were finishing up for the day when they heard a commotion from downstairs. Jay stored the paint in the closet and took the brushes to clean.

"That sounds like a woman on the warpath. I'm taking the chicken's way out and using the back door," Jay said as he stepped back into the room. Chloe joined him and the two left.

Josie glanced at Macy. "That leaves the two of us. Should we escape, too?"

They could hear raised voices.

Macy shook her head. "I want to see this."

They walked into the living room to see Avery Culpepper confronting Gabriel and Bea. The younger woman, in her 1970s version of country, was wearing big sunglasses, and her brass hair was pulled back with a headband.

"Miss Culpepper, I assure you, no one is trying to take away what is rightfully yours. And your grandfather was not an elderly man coerced into giving over his property," Bea soothed, but the tone didn't match the spark in her eyes.

"I don't know why you expect me to believe that. Here I am, his granddaughter, and I'm getting nothing but the runaround and questions about my identity. And you all are getting this house and hundreds of acres. For a boys ranch! And I know what the lawyer Mr. Phillips thinks of you all abandoning the ranch that his family donated. He isn't too happy about it."

Gabriel stepped forward. "Miss Culpepper, we're not abandoning the Silver Star. There are uses for both properties."

"Yeah, bringing in ruffians to thieve and vandalize." She flipped her hair over her shoulder. "I have to go, but I can guarantee you, this isn't over."

Gabriel motioned her toward the door. "Might I remind you that when this is over, if you stay here, these people will be your neighbors. So you might want to be careful how you treat people."

She flounced—that was the only word to describe it—out of the house. From the window they watched as she got in her convertible and sped off.

"Well, that was interesting." Josie stepped away from the window. "She does make an entrance. And an exit."

"I wish she would exit the whole area," Gabriel said.

Bea hushed him. "We'll get through this. The law is on our side. And, Macy, you are the person I came here looking for."

"Is Colby okay?"

Bea nodded and motioned for her to follow. "He is. As a matter of fact, we had a good conversation today, and there are some things you should know."

Her heart sank, but she followed Bea, taking some reassurance from the older woman's smile.

Bea led her to the kitchen. They still had some painting and cleaning to do, but the room was big and bright. It would serve the boys well.

"Sit down." Bea motioned to a step stool, and she grabbed one for herself, first putting the paint can on it down on the floor. "It's hard to believe we're days away from moving in here. But I've learned in life to not sweat the small stuff. What looks like a mountain in the distance is often just a bump in the road."

Macy sat and waited. She felt a little like she had in school when sent to the principal's office.

"Stop looking so worried," Bea ordered in a sweet but firm voice.

"But I am worried." So bothered that her hands trembled, and she clasped them together.

"Okay. I want you to know this because Colby is coming home this weekend for a pass. And it is not going to be easy for him, now that we've dredged up the past. Most specifically the night of his parents' accident."

Her heart trembled along with her hands. "Okay."

"Macy, they had a fight, before the babysitter got there. I don't think it was the end of the world, but to Colby it was. His mom was mad at him because he didn't want them to go out. She was mad at your brother, too. She said sometimes she wished she could just go away. It was probably one of those things a mom might say without thinking. But in this case, Colby's mom was mad, and she didn't come back. And then your fiancé, Bill, left."

"With the parting message that he didn't sign on to raise a kid."

"The two situations were just too much for a little guy to process."

Macy put a hand over her face and shook her head. Her poor little boy. "So how do I help him?"

"Love him. Be his mom. Let him talk. When he's afraid, don't discount his fear, just talk openly and honestly."

"I do love him, Bea. Sometimes I worry that I won't be able to help him."

"You're helping him. Being there for him is the way to help move him forward."

"Thank you, Bea. For everything you do for Colby and for the other boys."

"I love these kids, Macy. And their parents. That includes you."

She was a parent. Colby's parent. She reminded herself of that as she walked out the front door a short time later. She hoped she didn't let him down.

As she pulled her keys out of her purse, she became aware of someone standing on the porch. "Tanner."

"I've been waiting for you. I wanted to see if I could fix you dinner." He stepped out of the shadows, wanting to see for himself that she was okay.

"I…" She closed her eyes, took a deep breath and nodded. "I would love that."

"I thought you might not want to be alone."

She took his hand and he led her down the steps. "I would love for life to be less complicated. Just for a week or two."

He opened her car door for her. "It will be. And in the meantime, you're still moving forward."

"I am still moving forward," she agreed.

Instead of Tanner cooking, they stopped on their way back to town and took a pizza to Macy's. He parked his truck behind her car and followed her inside. The house had changed. Gone were the dark pictures on the walls. She'd replaced them with brighter colors. It was starting to feel like her home.

"Do you like it?" she asked.

"I do. It fits you."

He eyed the tubs and boxes. "Things you're getting rid of?"

"Yes. It's been difficult. I still have a drawer or two in their dresser that I just can't bring myself to open and look through. It feels too personal."

They walked into the kitchen, and she flipped on a light. Somewhere in the house he could hear the puppy barking. "Do you want me to let the puppy out?"

"Please. I have him kenneled in the spare room. Down the hall on the left."

He returned a few minutes later. "I put the

puppy in the backyard. And, Macy, if you want help sorting through things, I can do that."

"I know. And thank you. My mom is coming up in a few days. She said it is to see the new ranch and to help Colby with the transition back home. I think she's coming to see if she can talk me into bringing her grandson to live near her."

He opened the pizza box and took the plates she handed him. It wasn't the first time she'd mentioned Arizona. He had brushed it off, thinking it was just out of frustration, but saying it twice told him it meant something.

"Don't look at me like that," she said as she reached into the cabinet for glasses.

"Like what?"

"Like a storm cloud about to erupt." She poured him a glass of tea and then got herself water. She didn't ask, he noticed; she just knew.

And that troubled him, that she knew him so well, but she was thinking about leaving.

"I'm not erupting. I'm just hoping you don't go. I don't want you to go."

She opened the pizza box and put a slice on each of their plates. "I don't know what I want."

That didn't sound promising to a man who thought he'd like to be a bigger part of a woman's life.

"I don't mean it like that," she said. "I don't know, Tanner. I know what I want, but I'm afraid of what will happen. I'm afraid for Colby and myself. I'm afraid that I'll fail. I never planned to put myself in Cynthia's shoes. Even though we had discussed that they wanted to make me his guardian, I hadn't considered the reality of it. It wasn't supposed to happen this way. A guardian is a 'just in case.' And in this case, they had also considered the Wayes. And I wonder if they'd meant to change the will, to make them Colby's guardians."

"It's no use second-guessing the situation. You are Colby's guardian."

She leaned in close. "And I want to be his guardian."

"Life is messy," Tanner said. He picked up a napkin and wiped her chin. "And so are you."

She laughed and took the napkin from his hand. "I am a mess."

"Yes, but I kind of like the mess."

She pulled back and smiled up at him. "I kind of doubt that. I see you as a man who likes everything in its place. I'm chaos, at best."

"Chaos can be good." He leaned over, cupping her cheek in his hand as he lightly touched his lips to hers. The kiss was easy and sweet. He pulled back. "Yes, I like chaos. More than I ever dreamed possible."

His lips lingered over hers, and he pulled her

close. They ended up standing, her arms around his neck as he held her.

He didn't want to let her go. He wanted to convince her to give them a chance. But he also knew that she had to make her own decisions. As much as he'd like to sway her to stay, she would do what was best for her and Colby.

He'd never seen himself as the dramatic sort, but he kind of thought that their kiss felt like a goodbye.

Chapter Sixteen

Colby walked through the front door of the house on Friday afternoon, his overnight bag in his hand and an apprehensive look tugging at his mouth. When he saw his grandmother, he lost a little bit of that look and ran to her, letting her grab him up in a hug.

"Why, Colby, I think you've grown!" She held him up for inspection. "Yes, definitely a guy that could hike the Grand Canyon with me."

"Mom!"

Nora Lockwood smiled at her daughter. "Macy, I meant for a vacation."

"Thank you."

"But I did bring Colby a gift from Dr. Lock-wood." Nora spun Colby around again.

"You mean Granddad," Colby chided her. "That's what he likes to be called."

"Yes, Granddad."

But Macy's mom liked being a doctor's wife and so she often referred to William by his title. Dr. Lockwood.

"Oh, Macy, the title to the car."

Macy had forgotten. The minivan that had been Cynthia's. Her mom planned on selling it, and Macy had forgotten to look for the title.

"I think I know where it is." The drawer she hadn't wanted to deal with.

"Why don't you look while you're thinking about it? Colby and I have to plan a Grand vacation."

"Love the play on words, Mom." Macy kissed her mother's cheek and hugged Colby. "When you're done with the vacation planning, why don't you let Colby show you his room? We've been redecorating."

"I see that in the living room. Very colorful."

"Yes, I like color."

As she walked away, she heard Colby telling his grandmother about the new ranch. They were beginning the moving process. His cabin was being transitioned that weekend. But he wouldn't be there, because he was at home on a pass.

He sounded okay. She took a deep breath and prayed he would continue to move forward.

She headed to the back of the house and the bedroom she'd tried to avoid. In the top drawer of the dresser were papers she really needed to go through. She had to. And why not now?

There were bank papers, receipts. As she dug through, she found the car title. Simple. Easy. She should have done it months ago. She just hadn't wanted to do this. It seemed too final.

She started to put everything back, and she found a typed letter. She opened it and sat back to read. And reread.

The letter was typed on letterhead from Grant's office at school. There was no signature. But the desires of her brother and his wife were clear. Macy folded the letter and left the room. As she walked through the kitchen, she handed her mom the title of the car, and she grabbed her purse.

"Where are you going?"

"To town. I have to go to town." She shoved the letter in her purse.

"You can't just leave." Her mom stood, leaving Colby on the sofa, staring at the book on the Grand Canyon, his eyes big and luminous.

"Mom, I'm going to town." She gave a pointed look at the little boy. "I'll be right back. I'm not upset with anyone."

"Don't go, Aunt Macy."

She kneeled in front of her nephew. "Colby, when people leave, they also come back."

"Sometimes they don't," he whimpered.

"Of course they do. I'm coming back. Most important of all, I'm not upset with you or Grandma. I am a little upset about something I read, but that isn't your fault. You see, sometimes people are upset and say things, but they're not as mad as their words sound."

"God should have taken care of my mom and dad," he said.

"I agree. I wish He would have. And maybe He took care of them in a way we don't understand." She kissed his forehead. "Why don't you take Arthur outside? I'll be right back. And I'll even call in a few minutes to see if we need anything from the store."

Colby leaned his head on her shoulder. He was hers. No one would take him away from her. But what had her brother wanted? Had they meant to change their will and appoint the Wayes as guardians?

As she expected, her mom followed her to the door.

"Where are you going?"

"Mom, I found something, and I need to find out if it is recorded anywhere."

"What?"

She pulled the letter out of her purse and handed it to her mother. "It was in the dresser. I guess I should have cleaned it out sooner. I would have known sooner. But it makes sense."

Her mom shook her head as she read through the letter. "No, it doesn't. You saw the will. It named you as guardian. It gave you this house and the care of a child your brother and sister-in-law loved to distraction. They knew you would love him, as well. So, where are you going with this?"

"To the attorney in town, Mr. Haverman."

"Why? This isn't signed."

"But if he knew about it? What if they planned on changing their will and hadn't gotten around to it?"

Her mom put a hand on each of her shoulders and shook her head. "Mr. Haverman would have said something."

"Mom, I have to know. Maybe they hadn't talked to him yet."

"Okay, go, then. Just remember that you have a little boy counting on you to make choices that are best for him."

That took her by surprise. "I think having a real mom and dad would be best for him. So, Mom, what do you think is the best thing for Colby?"

Her mother smiled a secretive smile. "I'm not going to tell you, because I want you to make the decision you think is best."

"Okay, and thank you."

A few minutes later she pulled up in front of

Mr. Haverman's office. She got out, dreading what she'd discover. This letter could change everything. So why didn't she just throw it away and forget she'd ever seen it?

Because she wanted an out? She shook her head at the thought. No, she didn't. Maybe in the beginning when the speed bump looked like a mountain. But now? She'd adjusted. She could live in Haven. This could be her life.

She reached the door and pulled. It didn't budge. Of course it didn't. She found the hours posted and groaned. The hours showed that he went home early every Friday and he wouldn't be back until Tuesday.

"Problem?"

She turned, smiling at Chloe Barstow. "Yes. No." She shook her head.

"Maybe the problem is that you don't know the right answer."

"I found a letter."

She handed it over, and Chloe read it, not once but three times. "The Wayes?"

"Yes. I don't know what to do."

Chloe handed the letter back to her. "You take that to the nearest trash can and throw it away. It wasn't signed. It isn't legitimate."

"But is it what they wanted? What if that is what they were planning, and they just never got around to giving it to their lawyer?"

"What would it matter, Macy? You are the one who has been here for him. He needs you."

"But am I the best thing for him? I've watched the Waye family. They love each other. They love Colby. They have four kids and a minivan."

"But what does Colby want?"

"I'm sure he would pick a family with two parents and siblings. He always wants to be with them on Sundays."

"Why don't you ask him what makes him happy? I think he'll say you." Chloe walked with her back to the car. "And while you're asking, you might ask my brother. I think he would give you the same answer."

Macy called her mom and Colby on the way back to the house. They were laughing and talking about the puppy, and they informed Macy the only thing they needed was for her to not do the cooking.

On Saturday Macy and Colby sat down in the driveway to put together a new basketball goal. They had no idea what they were doing, but the picture on the box showed the base that would be filled with sand, the pole and at the top the backboard and hoop. Somehow it would all come together. Macy's mom was sitting in a lawn chair supervising. Arthur ran around the three of them, picking up pieces of paper and chewing them to bits.

"Shouldn't we read directions?" Colby asked. "My dad always told my mom to read the directions."

Macy drew in a breath, surprised by Colby's mention of his parents. "Did she ever read them?" *Keep it light*, she told herself. *Make it easy.*

"No, she never did."

"What happened?" Macy moved parts around, hoping she knew what went where.

"She could never put things together. Not even the Christmas tree. My dad laughed at her for putting it all wrong."

Memories. She smiled because Colby had them and they were good, and eventually he would learn to share them, and to treasure them.

"Did they get a picture of that tree?" Nora asked from her lawn chair.

Colby thought about that for a minute. "I think there is a picture."

"We will have to look for it," Nora pushed on. "I do love to look at pictures."

"I don't think I like pictures." Colby picked up a part to the basketball goal.

"Maybe when you decide, we can look for them."

He nodded and reached into the box for the instructions. "This looks complicated. You should read the instructions or call Tanner."

Heat crawled up her cheeks, and she put a finger to her mouth. Colby's eyes narrowed, and he shook his head.

"What?"

"Who is Tanner?" Nora asked.

"He kisses Aunt Macy," Colby supplied, all the while looking at the directions and pretending he wasn't causing trouble.

"He's a friend."

"Sounds like a friend," her mom said with a grin.

"So, back to this basketball goal." Macy handed a few parts to Colby. Maybe if she kept him busy, he wouldn't tell more than he had.

They worked for fifteen minutes, and what they had at the end of that time was...nothing. Macy sat back on her heels and stared at the mess. It looked like her life at this point. She couldn't do what needed to be done. She couldn't be a mom and a dad to Colby.

"I know that look on your face," her mom warned. "It's a basketball goal, Macy."

"It's something Colby wants. And I don't have a clue how to do it."

"You could call Mr. Waye," Colby offered. "He knows how to do all kinds of stuff like this."

Macy shot her mom a look. "Yes, I'm sure

he could. Mr. Waye is good at a lot of things, isn't he?"

"Yeah, but he can't cook. Mrs. Waye says he burns water."

"They're a pretty great family, aren't they?" she asked. And she wanted him to say they weren't. But she'd met them, and they were good people with a sweet family.

"Yeah, they are. My dad and mom used to like to eat dinner with them."

Macy's mom tapped her foot and then moved out of her chair to sit on the ground. "Grandma is going to have to show you all how to put this basketball goal together. You know, a long time ago I was all by myself, raising your dad and your aunt Macy."

"How come?" Colby asked.

"Because your grandfather, their dad, died. It was really tough. But we had each other."

"Like I have Aunt Macy?" Colby asked, fitting pieces together.

"Exactly like that." Nora handed him a part and took the directions from him. "Let's show your aunt what we can do."

"Hey, that's Tanner's truck coming up the road."

"Is it really?" Nora sat back and watched as the dark blue truck parked out front. "Maybe he can help us."

"Maybe." Colby jumped up and ran toward the parked truck and the man getting out of it.

Macy was tempted to do the same.

Tanner wasn't sure what to say to Macy. Chloe had let it slip about the letter she'd found. He couldn't believe she'd even think about handing Colby over to the Wayes. Even if she thought it might be best or what her brother had wanted. She had to know that her nephew had been through enough, and the person he wanted was her.

As he headed up the driveway with Colby talking a mile a minute about the basketball goal, his gaze tangled with hers. Once tangled, it was hard to disengage.

"Hello, you must be Tanner." An older woman with graying blond hair, clear green eyes and a mischievous smile stood to greet him. "I'm Nora Lockwood, Macy's mother."

"Good to meet you, ma'am." His gaze again clashed with Macy's. "Colby said you can't do this without me."

He leaned to pick up a part of the basketball goal.

"Help would be nice." Nora Lockwood moved from her chair. "And I think I'll go inside and see if we have lemons to make lemonade. Colby, come help me."

"We're going to make lemonade?" He jumped up to follow his grandma.

"I don't think we have lemons, Colby." Macy touched her nephew's arm. "But maybe you can find something in there."

Tanner started putting the pieces of the goal together. Macy sat back and watched.

"You know about the letter?" she asked.

"Chloe didn't mean to tell me. She was upset, thinking that you might consider giving Colby over to another family."

"The family my brother and his wife thought were better suited to raising him. Tanner, the letter was written just two months before..." She glanced away and swiped at her eye. "Before they died."

"I'm sorry." He kept working on the basketball goal. It was something he could do for her. Something he knew he could fix.

"They didn't want me. They wanted another family. People I didn't even know until I came here. And maybe they wanted the Waye family because they knew I wasn't ready for this. I'm not a mom. He needs a mom and a family."

He kept working. "You are his mom. I've watched you with him. And you are his family. You have your mom. You have the church and this community."

"What do I do with the letter? Pretend I didn't find it?"

"I guess you have to make that decision."

It *was* her decision to make. Not his. If it was up to him, she would never leave. She would stay and build a life for herself and her nephew.

He could admit, though, that he was a little selfish. He also wanted her to stay because he wanted her in his life.

"I do," she said quietly. "And it won't be easy. I never thought I would be in this place, making these decisions. What hurts is to think that you believe I'm being selfish, that this is about me, what I want. It isn't. It hasn't been about me since that night I stepped into this house and held my nephew as I explained that his mommy and daddy weren't coming home. It wasn't about me when I took him to Silver Star and left him. And this is not about me, because I want him to have the best home. Even if it means giving up."

"I know," he answered. The basketball goal was almost finished. He stood it up and finished the last pieces. "And maybe that's what you haven't considered. You are willing to give him up if that's what it takes to make him happy. I think that's the definition of a mother."

She lowered her head as tears streamed down her cheeks. "I would give up more than him."

"I guess you have decisions to make." He held

a hand out to her, and she took it, allowing him to pull her to her feet. "I know this isn't where you expected to be. But I hope that you decide it's where you want to be."

He rested his forehead against hers and held her loosely.

He moved, dropping a kiss on the top of her head. "And now I have to go, because I'm not going to stand here and beg you to stay in our lives."

The front door banged shut. Nora Lockwood came down off the porch, lips pursed and eyes narrowed. Macy stepped away from him, the distance between them feeling like miles instead of feet.

"What have you two done?" Macy's mom asked.

"We put the basketball goal together?" Macy responded, glancing at him, questions in her eyes.

"No, what did you say? Colby is inside upset because the two of you are fighting and it's his fault."

"It isn't his fault," Macy assured her mother as she headed for the house. "I'll talk to him."

Tanner watched her walk away. He felt a touch on his arm, hesitant and questioning.

"She can't give that boy up," Nora told him.

"I know. But she has to believe she can be a

mom. And she has to know that Grant and Cynthia picked her because they knew she was the best person to love their little boy." He pulled off his hat and brushed a hand through his hair. "If she doesn't believe that, there isn't much I can do to change her mind."

"I somehow doubt that," Macy's mom said as she picked up cardboard and packing materials.

He nodded and left, because he didn't know what else to say. He hadn't expected to be in this position, wanting her to stay and wanting to keep her in his life.

Chapter Seventeen

Macy had never suffered through such a long, agonizing weekend, followed by a longer Monday. She'd fought the urge to call Tanner. She'd avoided him by staying home from church. She'd spent the weekend talking to Colby about adults not always agreeing but that didn't mean they didn't still… She'd stopped herself from saying love.

Instead she told Colby how much she loved him.

She loved him enough to give him up if that was what was best for him. She sat in her car looking at Haverman's law office. She didn't want to go in. She didn't want to face the truth. Her brother and sister-in-law had intended for someone else to raise Colby. The thought settled deep inside like a lead weight.

What would she do if Haverman told her that

she needed to honor what had been Grant and Cynthia's last wish? All of this time she'd thought someone else would be better as Colby's mom. As his parents. She'd seen the Wayes with him, and it had seemed natural and loving.

But now, in her heart, Colby was hers.

Someone tapped on her car window. She jumped and then put a hand to her throat where her pulse beat at a crazy pace. Tanner motioned for her to put her window down.

She did. And then she couldn't speak. Her throat clogged with emotion, and tears burned her eyes.

"You're not really going to do this?" he asked, his mouth a tight and disapproving line.

"It isn't me doing this, Tanner. I want to know what my brother intended to happen."

"He intended for you to raise Colby. His will reflected that. This letter you found is not a reason for you to give up. You and Colby are a family. The two of you have bonded over the past year."

"I'm not giving up. I'm trying to do what is best for Colby."

"Is this about what is best for him?"

"You had to put the basketball goal together because I couldn't. Because my brother isn't here to do the things a dad should be doing. I'm not sure I can be a mom. I know I can't be a mom and a dad." Her heart cracked a little, thinking about all the things Grant wouldn't be there for. The things that Colby would miss out on with his dad.

"Yes, and I was there. Don't forget that part."

"I won't."

He backed away so she could get out of the car.

"They didn't sign the letter or give it to Haverman."

"Maybe they didn't have time?"

"Maybe they decided you were the best person to love him."

He walked away, and she whispered to his retreating back. "I think I might love you, too, Tanner."

She loved Tanner. She loved her nephew. So why in the world was she walking into a lawyer's office, intent on giving them all up? Because she wasn't sure her love was what they needed?

In the past year she'd felt like a failure on so many levels. Colby had needed her and she hadn't been able to help him. He hadn't felt safe with her. It made her question her ability to be a mom. If she couldn't rescue one little boy and make him feel loved, then how could she commit her life to being a mom?

She could let Colby go to the Wayes, and she could return to Dallas and visit him on weekends. Maybe he would be happier?

The receptionist in the wood-paneled office looked up, smiling from behind the glass partition. "Can I help you?"

Macy stood there wondering what to say to the question. Yes, she needed help. She needed answers. She needed to know that she was doing the right thing.

"I'm Macy Swanson. I'm here to see Mr. Haverman about my nephew, Colby Swanson. I don't have an appointment, but if he could just answer a question for me?"

The receptionist looked at her appointment book and nodded. "I'm sure he has a minute. Have a seat."

Macy wandered to the waiting area. Instead of sitting, she stood in front of the magazine rack. She closed her eyes and prayed, because she knew she couldn't do this on her own. She wanted to make the right decision. She wanted Colby to be healthy and happy.

She wanted to run after Tanner and tell him she was afraid, she couldn't be the person he wanted or needed. She didn't know anything about cows or horses, and it seemed that she didn't know much about children.

She knew books and libraries, how to teach and how to avoid the traffic during rush hour in Dallas.

She didn't want to let anyone else down. Her

mind flipped back in time, to the past year. To holding Colby during the funeral and then at night when he cried. They'd gotten through some tough times, she and that little boy.

They'd gotten through. The thought melted into her heart, chasing away the doubts that had plagued her for months. Her brother and sister-in-law had known. They hadn't taken this letter to Haverman. They hadn't changed their will. They had trusted her to raise their son. Maybe she was the one who needed to trust a little. Trust their decision. Trust her own abilities.

Maybe, rather than turning Colby over to the Waye family, she could invite them into her life.

It all made sense. She closed her eyes, thanking God for this answer when she needed it.

She pulled the unsigned letter from her purse, crumpled it and tossed it in the trash. As she walked out the door, the receptionist asked if she'd changed her mind or did she want to reschedule.

She shook her head and kept going. She'd not only changed her mind about seeing Haverman, she'd changed her mind about herself. She was much stronger than she'd given herself credit for.

Tanner walked back to Lila's, entering the crowded café and bakery and not really knowing why he was there. He saw Flint at a corner table. Flint waved Tanner over to join them.

"Flint?" Tanner pulled up a chair and sat down.

"I wanted you to know, I talked to my friend Heath Grayson. I think he's going to help us out with our vandalism."

A waitress hurried to their table, menus in her hand and a pot of coffee. "I just want coffee," Tanner told her. "I'm glad to hear that. We've got to do something before people start to believe Fletcher."

The waitress poured him a cup and hurried off.

"They found the Lawrences' horse this morning," Flint told him as they drank their coffee. "Grazing alongside the road about a mile from where the fence was cut."

"Glad they found him. Still doesn't explain how he came to be on the wrong side of the fence."

"No," Flint said, "it doesn't. But we're going to figure this out. It might take a while, but we'll get to the bottom of it."

"Before someone gets hurt, I hope." Tanner looked at the now-empty cup and searched for the waitress. She spotted him and headed their way to refill their cups. "About this friend of yours. Why hasn't he been around?"

Flint started to say something, but the waitress reappeared with two plates and more coffee. After she'd left, Flint dumped ketchup on his eggs.

"Just some old baggage. But I think he'll be fine. By the way, I saw Avery going into Fletcher's office. I think she's visited him a couple of times, and she's looking pretty proud of herself. If it was just her, I wouldn't worry." Flint stirred his eggs up and piled them on his toast. Tanner was starting to feel a little bit sick. Flint gave him a challenging look and then continued. "I worry that Fletcher will use her as a pawn to do his dirty work."

"He might, but we have a will and community support on our side. Fletcher might want to think about the fact that this community is his livelihood."

"I hope he is thinking," Flint said. "Bea has already taken a few new boys. We moved Cabin Two over to the Triple C. They're set up in their wing and we're moving Cabin Three today."

"That's good. Anything you all need over there?"

"Not that I know of right now." Flint forked up a big bite of the concoction.

"Then I think I'm going before I lose my appetite." Tanner pushed back his chair and stood. "I think I'll run out to the Triple C and look things over."

"We're having a dinner this weekend, a big cookout for the kids and the community." Flint leaned back in his chair.

"If you're making that public knowledge, then I would suggest you have the police on hand." Tanner didn't like thinking that way. But if someone wanted to cause problems, the cookout would be the time to do it.

He left and headed out to the ranch. When he got out of his truck, Colby, on a tire swing that hung from a big tree next to the house, saw him and came running. Another boy trailed along behind him.

"Tanner, we have new kids. And I have a cool room."

"Do you? How are you liking it here?"

"I like it a lot." Colby motioned the other kid forward. The boy was younger than Colby and obviously shy. He stayed back a few feet, dark-haired and dark eyes. He had a bruise across his cheek that was starting to fade.

"What's your friend's name?" Tanner asked.

"His name is TJ. He doesn't talk much. And we have another new boy named Danny. He's older than me. And he can ride a bike."

"Can't you ride a bike?"

Colby shook his head. "No. I just got a bike."

The boy didn't finish, and Tanner wasn't sure what to say.

"I'm sure you'll learn to ride it when you go home."

Colby shrugged, as if it didn't matter. "Yeah, I guess. I think Aunt Macy can teach me. I guess. If she stays. I think she wants to be in Dallas."

"I don't think so, Colby. I think she loves being here with you." And he was going to have a talk with her and let her know what her nephew was thinking.

"I like it okay on the ranch. I would miss Eleanor and Edward. And Miss Bea." Colby looked back at his new friend. "And TJ needs me around."

"Yeah, I'm sure he's glad you're here." Tanner patted Colby's shoulder and made an attempt at smiling, because a little boy shouldn't be okay with not going home. "You're a good man, Colby."

"Thanks, Tanner." The little boy beamed and suddenly looked older than his seven years. "I should go now. I have to show TJ all the stuff."

"Okay. Later, Colby."

Tanner headed for the barn. He knew Jay and other hands would be working, getting everything put away. He could help them out before he headed to his store. This would give him a chance to get to know Jay a little better, since it seemed he might be dating Chloe.

He had to give one to whoever was doing the

matchmaking. They'd saved his sister from a bad relationship, and they'd fixed her up with a decent guy.

That brought to mind a book and a note. The matchmaker's attempt to fix him up with Macy. It seemed they had failed when it came to Tanner and Macy. As much as he thought he might like her, he wasn't going to chase after her or beg her to stay in Haven.

He'd done enough begging in his life. Most of it before he turned ten.

What surprised him was how much he didn't want to walk away from her. All of the things he'd thought would be important in the woman he someday met didn't seem to matter. City or country, kids or no kids, he wanted Macy in his life.

But it seemed to him she was putting more distance between them, and that distance meant something. Maybe it meant she'd changed her mind about them. Maybe she meant to take Colby and go to Arizona.

Macy wasn't surprised to see Tanner's truck at the Triple C when she got there. She hoped she didn't run into him. Not now. Maybe after a few days, or a few weeks, she'd be able to talk to him, to tell him she'd made the right decision, throwing the letter away and choosing to stay.

She hadn't spoken to him since they met up outside Haverman's office.

Maybe he'd decided it was best to let her go, for them to go their separate ways. After all, they were two different people in different places. She had Colby to focus on. That had to be her priority. She'd received a call from Eleanor, telling her that today was the day she should move Colby home. He was getting too comfortable at the ranch and using it as a way to avoid his pain.

Macy understood wanting to avoid pain.

She walked into the ranch that smelled of new paint, something good cooking in the kitchen and fresh country air. Eleanor met her in the front living area. The other woman, her red hair held back with a headband, paint spattering her top, smiled and motioned her outside.

"He's on the tire swing with TJ," Eleanor told her as they walked down the front steps. "I didn't tell him that you were coming. I didn't want him to worry and get himself worked up."

"I understand. I've been working myself up on the drive over."

"Macy, you can do this."

"I know I can. I doubted myself for a while. But I'm not running."

As they crossed the yard, Colby waved and told Aunt Macy to come see the swing and meet his new friend. She smiled big, and when she got close, he ran to give her a hug.

"Colby, it looks like you're having fun." Macy waved to his friend TJ. The little boy, head down, started for the house.

"I didn't know you were coming to visit." Colby had her by the hand, pulling her toward the swing.

"Actually, this isn't really a visit, Colby," Eleanor cut in. "Aunt Macy is here to take you home."

Colby shook his head and pulled away from her. "I'm not going home. I want to stay here."

"Sweetie, what happened? I just don't know what to do. Grandma doesn't know what to do." Macy knelt in front of him, but he wouldn't look at her.

"I don't want any more people to get mad and go away. I don't want to go home. I can stay here, and you can go to Dallas if you want."

To Dallas. "What does that mean?"

"You told Tanner you don't think you can be my mom."

"I'm not going away," she said as firmly as she could. He had to believe her. "I'm here, and we're a family."

"You're not my mom." He cried as he said it.

She picked him up and sat him on the tire swing. "No, I'm not. I'm a poor substitute. I can't make chocolate chip cookies without burning them. I couldn't put together the basketball goal. I can't sing like your mom. But I love you. I'm not trying to take her place. I just want to be here with you."

He jumped down off the tire swing. "No, you don't!"

And then he ran off. Eleanor kept her from going after him.

"We'll try again."

"I don't think it's just about trying again," Macy said, watching her nephew round the corner of the house. "I think he needs to realize that I'm here and I'm not going anywhere."

"That's exactly what he needs from you."

"The two of us are a team, Colby and I."

Eleanor hugged her tight and released her. "We'll try again this weekend. And make sure he knows that."

"Thank you."

Dazed, she walked away. She had a cake at home and streamers hanging from the ceiling. She had bought the ingredients for his favorite casserole. Her mom had bought Colby a cool leash for Arthur.

And she was going home without him.

"Are you okay?" Tanner appeared at her side. She shook her head, feeling okay with the honest answer. "I will be. Colby isn't ready to go home with me. But I'm not giving up."

"Time," he started.

She cut him off. "I know, give him time. I will."

She wanted to ask if he would give her time and second chances. Maybe she didn't deserve either. And Colby needed her. Her nephew didn't need to be second in her life right now.

"Did you talk to Haverman?"

She shook her head. "I threw the letter away."

"Okay."

That was it. She didn't know what she expected him to say. But surely he could do better than that.

"I need to get home. My mom is waiting. We had a little family party planned. Balloons, cake, everything."

"The party will happen, Macy."

"I know it will. We've gone through so much and we'll go through more. But I think we're getting somewhere, and I do believe he'll come home."

He nodded and let her go.

She drove off with him in her rearview mirror. She didn't know what she'd expected. For him to declare his love and beg her to stay in Haven? To stay in his life?

He wasn't the kind of man who begged. And

she wasn't the kind of woman who begged. She'd learned more than just that she could be a mom. She'd learned that she was strong. She'd realized what she wanted for her life.

Chapter Eighteen

Saturday, the day of the party, was warm but breezy. Macy and her mom arrived early. They'd seen Colby every day since Tuesday. Each day he'd seemed to come around a bit more. He had seemed a little more sure of himself.

The cookout was being held on the big patio behind the house. The giant grill was going, and Flint and Jay were cooking burgers. Miss Bea waved and hurried their way.

"How are you, ladies?" Bea asked as she gave Macy a hug. "I have the best news. Samuel Teller will definitely be here for the reunion in March."

"That is good news. Two down, if we count Avery, and three to go. Has Flint made any inroads?"

"Not that I know of. But he does have a friend who is going to help out around here, making sure we don't have any more problems and trying to find the person responsible for all of our incidents."

"Who is his friend?" Josie Markham approached, her hand on her rounded belly.

"A Texas Ranger from Waco," Bea offered. "And speaking of Avery, that girl is a mess."

"I know," Macy confessed. "I almost wish I hadn't found her."

"But we had to. We'll let God take care of the rest," Bea assured Macy. "Now, you ladies go find something to eat. I think Colby is playing on the swings with some of the others. And we have boys who are giving their parents a tour of the new facility."

"How is Colby?" Macy asked. She'd seen him the previous day during counseling. It had been tough for both of them, but when she'd left, he'd given her a hug.

"He's good, Macy. We talked again this morning about trust. It's going to take time, and I think we should keep with our plan for him to have weekly counseling for a month or two."

"Thank you, Bea."

Macy left her mother with Bea and went in search of Colby. She'd been praying for him, that today would be the day. She knew the timing would eventually be right. She knew that Colby's heart would heal.

"Aunt Macy," Colby shouted and waved. He was on a board swing hung from a tree. "Want to swing with me?"

She did. Very much so. She approached, and he got up and gave her his spot. And then he climbed on her lap. She exaggerated a groan as he sat down. "Colby, you've grown."

"I know, I'm getting older and more mature. That's what Edward said. He said I would be a fine man and that you need me to be the man of the house. I told him I thought Tanner would be the man of the house. He laughed at that and said someone should tell Tanner."

"Oh, Colby." She buried her face in his back. "I'm so glad you're going home with me." She was so glad she was staying here with him.

A weight had been lifted this week. It had felt as if her heart had been waiting for her to come to terms with everything and to make a decision to stay in Haven with Colby. She felt more peace. She felt stronger.

Her mom had told her she'd been worrying too much about things that couldn't be changed and not moving forward with the life she had been given.

"You do like him, don't you?" Colby pushed with his feet, forcing her to set the swing in motion. "Because I think he likes you. And I don't want the two of you to fight."

"What?" She was yanked back to the conversation.

"Tanner," he said, as if it was a given. "I don't want the two of you to be mad at each other."

"Colby, people have disagreements sometimes. Remember when you were upset with me the other day?"

"Yeah."

"I came back."

They continued to swing in silence for a while. Finally Colby sighed and leaned back against her.

"Yeah, you came back."

"That's because I love you. Your mom and dad loved you, too."

"I keep waiting for them to come back. But they're not going to. It's just you and me now. And you aren't going anywhere, are you?"

"No, I'm not."

"For a while I thought you might." He broke her heart with those words. "I don't want you to go. Someday I'm going to call you Mom. Eleanor said I can."

"Of course you can." She squeezed her eyes closed, and it was just her, Colby, the autumn breeze and...

Tanner's cologne. She opened her eyes, and he

was standing by the tree, one shoulder against the rough bark of the big oak.

Colby stopped the swing and hopped down. "I have to go tell Grandma that I'm going home. Arthur will be glad."

"Yes, Arthur will."

Tanner moved away from the tree to the swing. He stood behind her, catching hold of the ropes and pulling back to set the swing in motion. They didn't speak. He continued to push. She flew through the air, every now and then catching his scent and the scent of autumn combined.

"I'm a little bit like Colby," he finally said. And he stopped the motion of the swing, pulling her back so that her head rested against his chest.

"How so?"

"I don't like to feel abandoned. I close off when I think people are walking away from me. And I won't beg someone to stay if they don't want to be in my life."

"I'm not going anywhere. Haven is Colby's home. It's my home," she said softly.

"That's the best news I've had, maybe ever." He moved to the front of the swing and reached for her hands to pull her to her feet. "Because I didn't know how empty my life was until you became a part of it. You and Colby."

He lowered his mouth to hers and kissed her long and sweet, holding her close and safe in his arms. She dug her toes into her shoes, needing to know the earth was still under her.

"Macy, I love you," he whispered close to her ear.

She grinned, turning her face into his neck. "That's the best news I've had, maybe ever."

"That wasn't the response I was looking for."

"I love you, too," she said as she closed her mouth over his for a brief moment to punctuate her words. "And I'm not going anywhere. I talked to Mr. Haverman this week. He said Grant approached him about the Wayes and had even talked to them, but then they decided to leave things as they stood because Colby is my nephew. He said they knew it would be tough, but that I could do it. Of course, they hadn't expected anything to happen."

"You're a good mom. It hasn't been easy, giving him space and adjusting to your new life here. I hope you know you're not in this alone."

"I know. I have my mom, Bea, Eleanor, the church…"

He pulled her close. "You have me."

"Yes, I have you. And I love you."

Tanner held Macy close for as long as he could. Because he loved her and she loved him. He hadn't expected to be sappy. He'd never been sappy in his life. But this woman changed things.

She made him want to write bad poetry and sing love songs.

He planned on telling her that. But not today. Today was about the ranch and about taking Colby home.

"Someday I'm going to ask you to marry me," he said as they walked back toward the house and the growing crowds of people.

"I think when you do, I'll say yes."

That was the way he wanted this day to go. He held her hand, and they found Colby telling his grandma that Tanner kissed Macy. And then he ran to tell Eleanor and Bea.

No one seemed too surprised.

* * * * *

If you liked this
LONE STAR COWBOY LEAGUE: BOYS
RANCH *novel, watch for the next book,*
THE RANGER'S TEXAS PROPOSAL
by Jessica Keller,
available November 2016.

And don't miss a single story in the
LONE STAR COWBOY LEAGUE:
BOYS RANCH *miniseries:*

Dear Reader,

I'm so glad to have another opportunity to participate in a continuity. Lone Star Cowboy League: Boys Ranch takes you to Haven, Texas, deep in the heart of Texas Hill Country.

The characters in this book quickly became special to me. There were moments that their journey took me by surprise. I hope that you'll love Macy, Tanner and Colby as much as I do and that the lessons they learn about grief, faith and finding peace will touch your heart and life.

I know from experience that there are so many children in placements like the LSCL Boys Ranch. They're waiting to go home, waiting to find homes and trying to find peace. If this book touches your heart, then allow your life to touch the lives of those children in the foster care system.

Brenda Minton

LARGER-PRINT BOOKS!

GET 2 FREE LARGER-PRINT NOVELS PLUS 2 FREE MYSTERY GIFTS

Love Inspired®

SUSPENSE

RIVETING INSPIRATIONAL ROMANCE

Larger-print novels are now available...

REQUEST YOUR FREE BOOKS!
2 FREE WHOLESOME ROMANCE NOVELS IN LARGER PRINT
PLUS 2 FREE MYSTERY GIFTS

HEARTWARMING™

Wholesome, tender romances

YES! Please send me 2 FREE Harlequin® Heartwarming Larger-Print novels and my 2 FREE mystery gifts (gifts worth about $10). After receiving them, if I don't wish to receive any more books, I can return the shipping statement marked "cancel." If I don't cancel, I will receive 4 brand-new larger-print novels every month and be billed just $5.24 per book in the U.S. or $5.99 per book in Canada. That's a savings of at least 19% off the cover price. It's quite a bargain! Shipping and handling is just 50¢ per book in the U.S. and 75¢ per book in Canada.* I understand that accepting the 2 free books and gifts places me under no obligation to buy anything. I can always return a shipment and cancel at any time. Even if I never buy another book, the two free books and gifts are mine to keep forever.

161/361 IDN GHX2

Name _____ (PLEASE PRINT)

Address _____ Apt. #

City _____ State/Prov. _____ Zip/Postal Code

Signature (if under 18, a parent or guardian must sign)

Mail to the **Reader Service:**
IN U.S.A.: P.O. Box 1867, Buffalo, NY 14240-1867
IN CANADA: P.O. Box 609, Fort Erie, Ontario L2A 5X3

* Terms and prices subject to change without notice. Prices do not include applicable taxes. Sales tax applicable in N.Y. Canadian residents will be charged applicable taxes. Offer not valid in Quebec. This offer is limited to one order per household. Not valid for current subscribers to Harlequin Heartwarming larger-print books. All orders subject to credit approval. Credit or debit balances in a customer's account(s) may be offset by any other outstanding balance owed by or to the customer. Please allow 4 to 6 weeks for delivery. Offer available while quantities last.

Your Privacy—The Reader Service is committed to protecting your privacy. Our Privacy Policy is available online at www.ReaderService.com or upon request from the Reader Service.

We make a portion of our mailing list available to reputable third parties that offer products we believe may interest you. If you prefer that we not exchange your name with third parties, or if you wish to clarify or modify your communication preferences, please visit us at www.ReaderService.com/consumerchoice or write to us at Reader Service Preference Service, P.O. Box 9062, Buffalo, NY 14240-9062. Include your complete name and address.

WESTERN WP PROMISES

YES! Please send me **The Western Promises Collection** in Larger Print. This collection begins with 3 FREE books and 2 FREE gifts (gifts valued at approx. $14.00 retail) in the first shipment, along with the other first 4 books from the collection! If I do not cancel, I will receive 8 monthly shipments until I have the entire 51-book Western Promises collection. I will receive 2 or 3 FREE books in each shipment and I will pay just $4.99 US/ $5.89 CDN for each of the other four books in each shipment, plus $2.99 for shipping and handling per shipment. *If I decide to keep the entire collection, I'll have paid for only 32 books, because 19 books are FREE! I understand that accepting the 3 free books and gifts places me under no obligation to buy anything. I can always return a shipment and cancel at any time. My free books and gifts are mine to keep no matter what I decide.

272 HCN 3070 472 HCN 3070

Name _____ (PLEASE PRINT) _____

Address _____ Apt. # _____

City _____ State/Prov. _____ Zip/Postal Code _____

Signature (if under 18, a parent or guardian must sign)

Mail to the **Reader Service:**
IN U.S.A.: P.O. Box 1867, Buffalo, NY 14240-1867
IN CANADA: P.O. Box 609, Fort Erie, Ontario L2A 5X3

* Terms and prices subject to change without notice. Prices do not include applicable taxes. Sales tax applicable in N.Y. Canadian residents will be charged applicable taxes. This offer is limited to one order per household. All orders subject to approval. Credit or debit balances in a customer's account(s) may be offset by any other outstanding balance owed by or to the customer. Please allow 4 to 6 weeks for delivery. Offer available while quantities last. Offer not available to Quebec residents.

WPBPA16R

READERSERVICE.COM

Manage your account online!

- Review your order history
- Manage your payments
- Update your address

We've designed the
Reader Service website
just for you.

Enjoy all the features!

- Discover new series available to you, and read excerpts from any series.
- Respond to mailings and special monthly offers.
- Connect with favorite authors at the blog.
- Browse the Bonus Bucks catalog and online-only exculsives.
- Share your feedback.

Visit us at:
ReaderService.com